LOVESICK

FOLIE À DEUX BOOK 1

CYNTHIA A. RODRIGUEZ

Lovesick

Copyright © 2019 Cynthia A. Rodriguez.

Cover Design by Kat Savage Designs of Savage Hart Book Services

Edited by Christina Hart of Savage Hart Book Services)

Formatted by J.R. Rogue

ALSO BY CYNTHIA A. RODRIGUEZ

NOVELS

The Sound of Serendipity

Evol

Insolent: A Dark Retelling

The Souls Duet:

When We Crash

Where We Fall

The Guiding Series:

Teófila's Guide to Saving the Sun

The Summer of Secrets Series:

Hate Me

POETRY

Dirty Hands, Broken Ribs, & Other Places My Heart Has Lived

For every single woman who has ever felt a little fucking crazy
(me included).

"But he that dares not grasp the thorn should never crave the rose."
— Anne Bronte

PROLOGUE
ABEL

I NEVER WANTED TO FLY.

It was never something I thought of whenever someone asked that stupid ass question about superpowers. You know the one.

"If you could have any superpower..."

The first thing that always popped into my mind was strength. I wanted to be the strongest man in the world. So I could hit my dad back when he knocked me around. So I could fight my ma off when she got into too much liquor and wanted to fuck me up a little.

Or a lot.

Next, I'd want to be invisible. So I could walk into stores and take what I want. So I could take care of myself so the hunger pangs didn't keep me up like they did most nights. So my ma couldn't get pissed about my eyes being blue and not brown like hers and my dad's. So I could live at my dad's house without him ever even knowing I'm there.

Like the secret he kept me as all along. I'd haunt his halls, just so I could feel a little bit of the love he gives his *real* family.

But flying? Never.

So how I ended up on the ledge of a twenty-second story window is something I'll never understand.

I could hear my ma now, her voice raspy from chain-smoking and screaming at me all damn day.

Do it. You're already here, idyot. *Everyone's watching you now.*

But I never wanted to fly, Ma.

And I never wanted so many fucking eyes on me.

There are TV crews and cops and fire trucks, and I feel like something just snapped me back into consciousness, with the world staring up at me while my toes hang dangerously over the ledge. The wind is different up here, more violent, threatening to push me over. And I'm scared as fuck.

"Don't worry, son. We'll get you the help you need," someone is yelling from the window beside me.

But he doesn't know that I don't need any fucking help.

I just need to get my ass down from this fucking window.

1 ROSE

EYES ARE TRICKY THINGS. SPINDLY LITTLE VEINS decorate each pair and, though the thought is foolish, I've had enough eyes on me to know that those veins reach out like branches and come close to physical contact. Some stares touch you, hold you.

Some are more binding than any straitjacket.

Thankfully, I'm not wearing one today.

The eyes on me appraise me in this torturous solitude, and I stare back, pushing against their comfort from behind the door the best way I know how. There's only a small opening, making it impossible for me to see anything other than those exacting eyes.

I hope mine reach out and touch them.

I hope the touch scares them. Hurts them.

And when they run back to report, I hope they shudder, just enough that the hair on their arms stands on end.

A slight squint is all I get and then they're sliding the opening shut.

I didn't always like the way people looked at me. I especially didn't like how I could read exactly what they were thinking when they were looking at me. I used to think I could read minds but when I discovered it was my voice in my head telling me everything, I realized I was just reading their body language and filling in the blanks.

Thirteen, fourteen.

Oftentimes I think I'm a genius.

Until I do something incredibly reckless like stabbing Barb in the arm with the sharp edge of the plastic fork that I kept in my waistband, before they took it away. All because she kept interrupting the game of tic tac toe I was playing with Allison. But Barb and Allison aren't in confinement, I am. I should've learned my lesson last time, but the anger runs too hot for me to keep it contained like a bottle with its top secured tightly. It was a futile fight, trying to keep it within when it won every time.

So perhaps I'm not a genius. Perhaps I am my emotions' slave; chained and whipped into improper action.

Twenty-seven, twenty-eight.

I look down at my arms, covered in and pocked with the marks the nurses left, whether a few hours ago or in the three years I've been here. I don't understand why they don't try to use their words first.

But when it's time to assist, it's usually past the point of words if I'm involved.

Still, they don't politely escort anyone anywhere. The moment we pass through those doors, before the ink has even permanently ebbed itself in the documents keeping us here, we are no longer deemed fit to experience even a touch of respect. They grab you and drag you in a weak attempt to enforce their power and all the while, I'm hearing what they're thinking.

She's insane.

Don't let her get too close.

Don't become her next victim.

I can see it in the narrowing of their eyes; the way they hesitate to touch me. They've seen what I'm capable of. They've been briefed.

I've just hit four hours when the door opens, the sound of the uneven bottom scraping at the dry concrete. It's jarring after so long in silence and I'm sure my visitor witnessed the flinch I attempted to hide, as if I were only adjusting myself.

Comfort is something I'd lose myself in trying to find. An ever-evasive foe.

"How are we doing, Ms. Montgomery?"

Meant to sound warm, all his voice does is grate at my annoyance. And annoyance leads to anger and anger leads to people getting hurt or killed and scrubbing blood from my violent hands. I keep my eyes trained on present company in an attempt to keep from checking if they'd cleaned the blood from beneath my nails. The way they'd scrubbed was enough to make it so my hands were still feeling slightly burned.

"Speaking French again, Joe?" I try for casual. Faking it so I can stand to be in this dank room with this incompetent man.

I hate his name. It's so dull. Even his last name is dull. Brown. Joe Brown.

"Funny that you mention it," he starts, "I'm nearly fluent in French."

"*Tu es bête comme tes pieds,*" I say as he rifles through the pages on his clipboard.

He offers a small smile and a nod.

I'd spent too many springs coasting along the French Riviera to give Joe the satisfaction of thinking that I was beneath him in any way.

Joe. I want to roll my eyes. Many sessions I have to fight myself to keep from asking him who hated him enough to name him.

He sounds like he lives vicariously through people. That's probably why he insists on acting like we've been stuck in this box of a room, speaking French and counting together.

"How long have you been in here?" He settles the edge of his clipboard into his stomach, holding the other end in his hands so it juts out toward me.

"Four hours, three minutes, and thirty-six seconds." My words are low, but clear. If there's anything in the world my mother hated, it was when I mumbled. So I got in the habit of clearly enunciating every single thing I say.

"I heard you had another violent outburst." His voice slices through the bubble I try to build around myself. Almost conspiratorially, like we're friends sharing secrets.

I'm starting to wish for punishing solitude.

I don't know that I'm like others. When I hear a sentence, the unimportant words fall to the wayside and I hone in on the word that sticks out most to me. In this case, I hate that he says "another", as if I need to be reminded of the moments and experiences that led to my imprisonment. He'd never let me forget even a second of it. I have years behind me. I still have decades left in here to have my actions drilled in my head relentlessly. There is no room to forget; certainly not in this snug little room that smells like bleach and urine, each inhale costing me a little more of one of my senses.

In all my years here, there's one emotion I've yet to experience. The nurses used to watch me closely when I first got here, as if I should have been drowning in my regret over the things the news said about me; the things they'd read in my files. It only took biting one of them to get them to stand a little farther from me and to completely avoid eye contact.

"Did you hear Barbra needed stitches?" he asks.

He shoves his hands in his pockets and I fight the recurring urge to roll my eyes. My eighteenth birthday is only a few days away and it's a goal of mine to be treated like an adult. So I have to act like one.

"You know I haven't heard anything, Joe," I tell him slowly, carefully, as I glance around the room to remind him that this is where I've been.

At least he isn't writing on that clipboard of his. He hesitates before he steps closer to me, presses his clipboard against his chest, and looks directly in my eyes. *Doesn't he know I bit one of his nurses for a less direct stare?*

"And you feel no remorse?" His question is a whisper and he steps back to look down at his clipboard. It's a question he's asked too many times to count.

My answer is always the same. "I'm not familiar with that emotion." Bored, I start to pick at my split ends. I never knew what made them so terrible until I got here, my ends drying up and tangling with ease. Mother always made sure I was groomed to perfection. I'm sure if she saw my nail beds now, she'd have a stroke.

Then again, I doubt she'd care. I haven't seen any of my family members since I was signed in, though my mother *should* stay away. Still, almost two birthdays have passed with nothing from Grace.

Will I ever see my sister again?

"Rosamunde?"

I sigh and look up at the doctor, my brow arching. "Yes?"

"I know you think you're correcting people but you have to know you aren't an enforcer of right and wrong..."

Because apparently my moral compass is shot.

"...and this isn't a typical social setting. These patients don't realize what they're doing or how they're treating others."

"And yet someone still punished them by putting them in here." I tuck my hair behind both ears. "Unless you'd like to take responsibility for how they are now, Joe."

Joe isn't paying my response any attention as he shuffles through the pages on his clipboard. "Look, I can try to get you out of here in a few hours if you promise to work on this. You can't go harming other patients again. If we're preparing you for the day you get out of here, that doesn't fly out there either."

His argument makes me squint. It's hard to believe this man has a thorough education.

"I'm not getting out of here any time soon. By the time I leave, you'll be retired. Maybe even dead," I say.

He grimaces and I nod.

"So don't attempt to fill me with this false sense of hope. That's the kind of thing that makes me violent," I say.

"Rose, just tell me you'll work on it so I can get you out of here before you count yourself to death."

The amusement I hear in his tone has my skin growing warm, the lava beneath my surface churning and rolling with an increasing need to be free.

Unlikely, I want to tell him, but instead I tell him what he wants to hear for once. I hate solitary so much; it beats me down and makes me passive.

"I will," I lie.

"That's all I needed to hear," he says before placing his hand on my shoulder.

I hate that insincere touch but I let him keep his hand there for a moment. Anything to get out of here.

In another life, when I'd been able to watch movies, I caught a showing of *The Hulk*. The redundancy of Marvel's take on a Jekyll and Hyde storyline almost had me impatient to change the channel.

But the way Bruce Banner eventually embraced the monster—in a way Dr. Jekyll never really did—fascinated me.

Don't make me angry. You won't like me when I'm angry.

I smile at the way those words stick and Mr. Brown smiles back. I look away like the rebellious caged animal that I am, refusing to perform for the master.

In truth, part of me feels liberated in here.

My demons have a playground; one where I'm not the only one who doesn't play by the same rules as the other kids.

In my last life, I'd been forced to be Dr. Jekyll. Bruce Banner.

In this life, I'm only ever the monster.

He steps out and I'm right back to counting.

One, two, three.

It's only after three hours that Mr. Hyde is let out to mingle with the rest of the monsters.

2 ABEL

IT TURNS OUT, IT ISN'T A CRIME TO ALMOST JUMP OFF A building.

But it sure as fuck isn't something people just let you walk away from.

Where would I have even walked away to?

While I didn't necessarily enjoy my time living in my shitbox of a car, watching it get towed away wasn't something I'd been prepared to face.

That car was my goddamn home.

I now dub that incident as "the beginning of the end" because hours after they took my car, I found myself getting rescued from the edge of death.

"I understand you are homeless."

I don't think it's meant to be a question, but it kinda sounds like one. The woman in front of me stares at me and I stare at the wall behind her.

"Mr. Sommerfeldt?"

"Wasn't sure if that was a question," I say with a sigh, crossing my arms. At least they don't think I'm crazy enough to be shackled or in some fucking straitjacket.

"It was implied."

"Was it?"

She doesn't answer, only pinches her thin ass lips together.

"*That* was a question," I whisper.

"So, you have no next of kin to call, and no home." She's writing things down on that notepad of hers and I like to think I can be a nice fucking guy but this chick and her not-so-obvious questions are getting on my nerves.

"Sorry, but do you know when they're gonna feed me?" I glance at the white door with its tiny window to remind me that I'm not exactly here by choice. No one stands outside the door, I hear nothing other than the sound of her writing whatever bullshit she needs to in order to release me.

But it's like someone's breathing down my neck. *Go away, go away.* I close my eyes, squeezing them, trying to get rid of this feeling. I open them when I don't hear the pen scratching the paper anymore.

She's staring at me over her tiny ass glasses.

The word "spectacles" comes to mind.

She still hasn't answered me.

"That was also a question," I mutter as I sag back against the chair I'm sitting in.

"I'm getting the sense that you aren't taking this seriously. It's unfortunate." She places her one hand on top of the other, her pen still in her grip.

"Shit, I mean, it isn't like I have much to say, lady. I don't remember how I got up there. You're wasting your time here. I'm not some crazy person." I try not to look around the room, and I barely give this woman my eyes. I need to be in control.

"I can't, in good faith, release you, Mr. Sommerfeldt. Not without your cooperation," she says as she looks over the top of her glasses at the paperwork beside her. "You are a danger to yourself. And you may very well be a danger to the public with the stunt you pulled."

"I'm pretty damn sure you can't talk to me like that." I scoot the chair back, almost on my feet, ready to walk right out of here, but her next words have me planting my ass right back down.

"Best you settle down before I have you sedated."

"Ma'am," I start, but she's already gathering her things. "You're really gonna waste taxpayers' dollars over this bullshit?"

I watch as she removes her glasses with a sigh. Her fingers reach up to pinch the bridge of her nose and, after a deep breath, she regards me. "Abel, am I the only person in the room with you right now?"

I can hardly get a fucking word out for all the sputtering I'm doing. *This bitch. How? How could she...*

"Unfortunately, you've wasted all the time I had, being a wise ass. So, I have no choice but to commit you, where you can get the help you need. And I have the perfect place in mind."

"You can't commit me!"

She knocks on the door and a man I didn't know was standing there opens it. "Watch me."

I hadn't noticed the sound of the door locking when I came in.

But that shit was loud and clear after it closed behind her.

3 ROSE

I turned eighteen two days ago. The only person to wish me a happy birthday was Joe.

He remembers everyone's birthday, even the janitors'.

All of these special days and mine didn't count to anyone other than the man that lied about speaking French.

Crétin.

I wasn't a genius on my birthday.

I was imbecilely hopped up on hope and because I wrestled with keeping the violence from its inevitable and magnificent eruption, I ended up in solitary. Which is where I am now, the bleach and urine welcoming me back with the singeing scent of a poor cleaning job.

There's still blood on my shirt. If I bring my shirt close enough, I can smell it; its metallic tang kicking my inner nostrils a little differently than the room's scent. My mind is still reeling from the sweet release of anger, hot and spurting out of me like blood from an artery. I imagine this release is my highest high.

Causing pain makes me feel like I have control. I feel, you feel. I hurt, you hurt. I stab, you bleed.

Joe came in when I was already two hours into solitary, asking me how long I'd been in here and if I'd work on myself.

No. "I'm not apologetic," I tell him. "I don't want to change and I don't want to be 'better'." Because of that, I am still in this box. No one breaks up the time; no one checks in. I stop counting once I hit thirty-six hours.

Joe likes that he thinks he knows me so well, with his titles and names for what he thinks is wrong with me. For knowing that I count.

In an effort to become unrecognizable, I lie down on the floor and sleep.

Now I'm not sure how long I've been here.

I don't know anything except the sounds of the violent turmoil that landed me in here.

I'm not sure I'm so intelligent anymore.

Wait.

I know I don't want to spend another birthday at Silverwing.

I'll end my own life before that happens.

"Rose?"

I open my eyes but I don't sit up and I don't face Joe. I'm hoping that if I annoy him, he'll keep the nurses from force-feeding me, he'll stop wasting sedatives on me and I'll just die right here on the rough tiles, soaked in terrible scents. Any way to get out of here.

I don't know how many days it's been but I know I haven't eaten during any of them, a bold venture since I know the feeding tube will show up at some point. I haven't showered. I've willed myself to sleep as often as I can on this hard floor.

I want to rebel against my plan and this place. I want to stand and rip Joe's eyes from their sockets. I want to yank him inside and lock him in this room with me as I tear into his soft flesh with one of the fancy engraved pens he keeps in his left breast pocket. Directly over his heart.

My plan keeps me from doing anything but lying there.

Hope is a wicked thing. Hope macerates the genius in me.

"Rose, are you ready to talk about this?"

No.

"Don't you want to leave this room?"

And abandon the puddle of urine that's been keeping me company?

I *am* an animal. They keep me in this room like a feral dog in a kennel. They are afraid of me so they subdue me with their drugs and they think they can control me. They weaken me and poke and prod at me but I will never fold again.

"You have to eat, Rose."

Or you'll use a tube to feed me again? Part of me almost turns to talk. I hate the feeding tube.

He remains by the door.

Maybe Joe *does* know a thing or two about me.

"Are you upset with me, Rosamunde? Are you awake?"

Finally—because I am eighteen, after all—I turn onto my back. I don't speak but at least he can see I'm awake, that way I can tell him I do not consent to the feeding tube. It'll be too late to speak because my lack of consent never stops them.

We don't need your consent anymore, their eyes say. Something else left at the front door beside my forgotten respect. My consent now kept it company, both waiting for the day I walk out of here.

They wait in vain, according to Dr. Brown.

"If I get you out of here, will you eat? And continue your medication? It isn't good for you to stop taking them, cold turkey."

Oh, this faux concern.

I haven't taken my medication in years. I store the pills in my cheek, against my gums, so when they check, they don't see them. Then I spit them out in the bathroom and eat the bland oatmeal they peddle for breakfast.

"Don't you have anything to say?"

I stare at the high, speckled ceiling, wishing I could somehow launch through it, back to freedom. I think of all the things I'd love right now. A cheeseburger and a bazooka immediately come to mind. Extra pickles on the former.

Given the chance, I'd aim the latter right at this building and smile as it decimates the place that punishes me for being myself.

Growing up, my teachers would always tell me to be myself. To never change to try to fit in. "Be who you are," they said. "You were born to stand out."

I took those words to heart, never understanding that as long as you followed the standards set in place by society, you'd be accepted. Being myself used to be conditional in the real world. And then I came here and I was no longer offered even the possibility of being an individual. I wear the same clothes every other patient does: blue scrubs with no shape and no drawstrings, and thick socks that catch all the dirt on the floor. I am another number to them, a percent, a cow in their rotation of livestock. So when I turn to face Joe, I can only think of one message I'd like to convey after sitting in this room that was engineered to break me.

"I would like to no longer be an object you own."

4 ABEL

I HAVEN'T JERKED OFF IN A WEEK AND A HALF.

A whole fucking *week and a half.*

One of my favorite pastimes, on its way to being long fucking forgotten.

You'll go blind, I could hear my ma nag.

"Fuck off," I grunt into my pillow.

In a few days, I'll be transferred to an inpatient ward, among the other freaks and psychos.

Meanwhile, I can't even manage getting a chubby these days, not even a good ol' morning wood. It's too cold, my hands are too dry, and I don't have a fucking *lick* of privacy here. They keep my goddamn door open all day, force me out of my cot and into little therapy groups every hour, and check on me multiple times a night.

It's the worst cockblock of my entire existence.

On the other hand, I could be worrying about my next meal instead. Or how I'd manage to stay warm in my car all night.

Perspective, I think to myself as I roll over in this hard ass cot. Footsteps come down the hall, and just for the hell of it, I stick my hands down my pants.

The sound of hands clapping together makes me jump.

"None of that, you. Or I'll have you put away."

I don't know what that shit means but it's enough for me to quit dicking around, even if the smirk on my face doesn't quite match the action.

Wherever I end up, it *can't* be any fucking worse than this place.

Whatever this place is, anyway.

5 ROSE

TIME PASSES LIKE WATER THROUGH MY FINGERS. No matter how much I count, no matter how hard I try to keep track of it, it escapes me.

I stare down at my palms in my lap in my defeat for a moment. Time feels like it stops in this dreaded room during these stifling conversations, but that's a fallacy. It continues, stretching thin during these sessions but never stopping completely.

Not even for me.

Time will not heel to my violence.

My eyes catch on the calendar hanging up on Joe's wall. He's stopped his relentless speaking to respond to an email, something he rarely does. But I've taken this time away from his microscope-like gaze to examine the room.

It felt like I'd turned eighteen only a few weeks ago.

I shrivel back when I realize that, no, it hadn't been a few weeks, but closer to a year.

Today, I am not myself. Today, I am some sort of Bruce Banner, sullen and so inside myself that maybe I'm the only casualty of that anger that hasn't reacted in so long. I wonder if my monster is asleep or simply dead forever.

"Well, I have to say that I'm happy we haven't had an incident from you in some time."

I don't respond—verbally or nonverbally—my eyes still on the calendar.

What would the point be?

He's set his laptop aside and those intrusive brown irises are back on me, sizing me up, attempting to understand me, wanting to dissect me.

But there *is* no understanding me.

We are wasting our time here.

"Is there anything you'd like to say, Rosamunde?" He leans forward and braces himself on his elbows. "You've been awfully quiet this session."

I want to laugh, a dry chuckle laced with confusion and annoyance. "Is that not what you want? What you and your staff have attempted to do all this time? Take my anger, beat it out of me, silence me, make me a mummy like everyone else here?" The words started out quiet and clear but ended with my teeth bared.

He shakes his head and the look in his eyes makes me want to scream.

There she is, they say to me. *There's the monster.*

"I will never win here," I whisper, my eyes filling.

"What is it you think winning means?"

The sigh released from my parted lips is choppy and pregnant with an emotion that threatens to strangle me. "Freedom."

He doesn't say it, but the little shake of his head tells me what I feared.

There is no freedom for you, Rosamunde Montgomery.

Hell is your home.

6 ABEL

I'D NEVER BEEN PLACED IN CUFFS BEFORE TODAY. Something I was more than proud of, given the life I'd been living on the streets.

It wasn't that I never did anything *worthy* of cuffs, it was that I was too smart. Too street smart, too quick, too slick to get caught when it was time to steal dinner or snag a pair of shoes because the ones I owned looked like they could talk when I walked.

But all that shit went to hell when they cuffed me—chains and all, like I was some kind of fucking criminal—and placed me in the back of this van.

I'd guess the ride was about an hour from the last place to here, and when they finally open the van doors, my eyes squint at all the green. So many damn trees and nothing else for miles.

Smart.

Someone in a shitty green shirt walks up, pens lined in his breast pocket, a look of eagerness in his eyes.

Fucking weirdo.

And they lock *me* up?

"For God's sake, remove the cuffs." He watches as my escorts unlock them and part of me wants to shake this man's hand. "He isn't a criminal."

Not today, anyway.

He runs his hands over his brown hair, like he's nervous or something. That same hand hits my shoulder, not hard, but enough for me to look at it, then back at him.

"I'm Dr. Brown. Welcome to Silverwing."

I don't plan on speaking. I need to play my cards right if I want to get out of this place as soon as fucking possible. So I nod and let him lead me inside. The escorts follow us in, one in front of me, one behind me, blocking my view of any codes being entered and keeping me far enough away from Dr. Brown should I decide to fucking kill him, I guess.

We walk through the facility and he talks and talks before I'm handed clothes to change into. From one pair of shitty feeling clothes, to another. These are rougher on my skin, though. Not surprising, seeing as this place seems to be a step down from where I was.

Fuck.

I pull my pants up and the escorts are on me, patting me down before nodding.

And I guess the transaction is complete because now it's just me and Dr. Brown.

This fucking guy is going on and on and I'm trying hard not to tell him to get the fuck away from me. I've had it with strangers touching me and leading me places. But I don't because at least I don't have cuffs on anymore. His shirt is the color of baby shit, but I try not to hold that against him. It'd be easier if he just stopped talking and left me alone.

It's cold here and the hallways smell like vomit. The look on the nurses' faces tell me I've just walked into a real shit show. Ma would've called it hell but, I could always be in prison with a shank between my ribs and a dick in my mouth. Not that the last two things have happened but there's always the fucking possibility.

I shudder at the thought and glance at the doctor to see if he noticed but he's so invested in his welcome speech that he doesn't miss a beat. Then again, he's probably seen some really weird shit, considering his line of work.

He leads me into the rec room and I expect it to look like it does on TV. Like a bunch of old people and a lady with a baby doll that she swears up and down is real. But it isn't like that. It's worse.

Almost everyone looks brain dead and there's only one TV, the volume low and the image unclear. Other than a few ratty game boards, these people have no other way of entertaining themselves.

I look over every face, trying not to let the blank stares get to me.

Think of the shank and the dick and the cuffs, Abel. Well, not dick. *Don't think of that, ever.*

Unless it's yours in a hot chick. That's acceptable.

Everyone's sitting except one person.

She's walking around the perimeter of the room and though she's just hit the opposite corner, I still feel her stare like a hot fucking poker.

She sticks out like she doesn't belong here. Her hair is too blonde, her eyes too mischievous, her lips too pretty and pink. She's fucking gorgeous.

And she's more alive than anyone I've seen in a long time.

I've seen women that made me double take. Women I'd give one of my nuts to fuck. She's beautiful but when she looks away, I notice the way her clothes hang off her body and the marks that track her arms. Her movements are jerky, and I bet she has no idea.

Like she's had to protect herself for a really long time.

The thought makes me rub the back of my neck.

She probably has no idea that I'm watching her like I'm getting fucking paid to.

Ma used to tell me that she prayed forty days in a row before my due date for my *basherte*. She used to tell me God had already picked out my soul mate those forty days before I was born. But when she didn't go into labor until a few days after her due date, she just figured God needed extra time with her, to make her perfect.

She said that was when she knew I'd be in a pain in the ass. *A bi gezunt,* she'd say. *So long as you're healthy.*

I never really paid Ma any attention. She was too drunk to understand most days and when she'd finally sober up, her violent outbursts made her fucking impossible to live peacefully with. Rarely did she have a good day. But I'll always remember the way her eyes filled when she talked about *basherte* and the possibilities.

I think she thought my dad was supposed to be hers.

Instead, she died with a bottle in her hand and that glassy look of shit hope in her eyes.

Eyes unlike the ones I'm looking at, now that she's looking my way again. So bright and invading; they cement my feet to the ground and I'm momentarily fucking paralyzed.

I look away first because Dr. Brown is saying my name.

He follows where I was staring and gives me a quick nod.

"Be careful with that one. She's one of our more violent patients."

My eyes flicker to her once more at his words. She has her back to us and she's still walking. I can just make out the soft curve of her jaw when she tucks her hair behind her ear. When I look back at Dr. Brown, his eyes are on her too. He isn't looking at her the way I am, though. Not the way a man looks at a woman, thank fuck.

But I still don't like the look in his eyes.

He looks at her like she's a lost cause, with a shake of his head and a quick dismissal.

No one should be looked at like that.

I've been on the receiving end of one of those looks and it leaves you feeling shitty and unable to do anything about it. It gives your hope the kiss of death.

"So, our first session will be tomorrow, around eleven. I've got a meeting to get to, but the staff will take very good care of you."

He's walking away before I can say anything, and I grab one of the plastic chairs at the nearest table and sink into it. The woman a few chairs away doesn't acknowledge me at all. No one does, not really. Time ticks on and my leg shakes with impatience. I can't hear the TV from here, but I can't get a good look at what's on anyway. This has to be what makes people go crazy, having to sit here and do nothing. And this is my life now.

7 ROSE

SOMEONE NEW IS HERE TODAY. I HAVE NO IDEA HOW this person ended up here—their gender, their age...nothing. I only see the same white van that brought me here, sitting outside the entrance. Before I can get a look, the nurses clear their throats and exercise as much force as they can without causing a disturbance.

Without forcing *me* to cause a disturbance.

I back away from the barred window just as escorts get out and open the passenger door, keeping my eyes on them for as long as I can, until all I can see is wall and then the cheap, dingy linoleum under my feet as I walk toward an empty table.

Welcome to the cattle farm. Try not to go crazy.

Allison looks at me and I shake my head. I ignore the way her face falls. Truthfully, I'm not in the mood for her enthusiastic attitude; the way saliva pools at the corners of her lips and she lisps. Every time she speaks, I worry that this is the day I'll be wearing her spittle on my face.

That'll be the day Allison no longer looks at me with anything other than fear.

I stare longingly at the door. Waiting. Hoping.

It's a feeling I haven't been acquainted with in a very long time, the foreign feeling sitting on my shoulders before sliding its way down to my stomach.

I secretly want the new patient to be my age because I'm sick of the fact that the person closest to eighteen is thirty-one and randomly shrieks from time to time, making any sort of interaction impossible. Her random outbursts make me want to shove a pair of socks in her mouth. Maybe place my pillow over her head and press until her last breath gives out from her lifeless body.

Joe has a point, though. I shouldn't treat her like she's being rude just because she won't let me complete a full sentence before she starts yelling. This is what he's been filling my head with since my last stint in solitary after my birthday.

Still, I bet it would feel good to silence her screams. Perhaps even give her a real reason to scream. I mull these thoughts over as I get up and walk around the rec room, ignoring Allison, who keeps trying to wave me over. I glance her way to see her talking to the empty space beside her. Her ratty ponytail, full of coarse dark hair, doesn't move while she speaks enthusiastically to her own demons. Before she can catch me staring, I look away. She bores me. Everyone in here bores me.

Still, the nurses pay me extra attention. They think I can't feel their stares, like I can't read their minds.

Better be careful. Don't get too close.

The doors open, and I don't bother looking because everything is the same as yesterday and the day before and my hope is an angel on my shoulder that will soon fall like Lucifer.

I'm restless. I'm a prisoner.

I'm a slave to my violence and my boredom.

I hear Joe and can't help but look his way because he's hardly ever in the rec room. Unless…

I see the crisp olive button-up shirt Joe always wears on Tuesdays.

My eyes skate over Joe's graying hair and are drawn to the person he's speaking to.

Bright blue eyes a bit sunken, skin a little pale, hair the color of mud. The sight of him is as strong and shocking as a gut punch.

I imagine this is how Lucifer felt when he fell. That sweet fear mingled with weightless euphoria as gravity pulls your body toward your world's center.

He must've fallen with a smile on his face.

Is it my boredom? Or his looks that can't quite be classified as handsome? His sinister features intrigue me.

I'd like to be perfect for a moment just to be ruined by him. I'd hand him my crooked tiara and watch him break it.

Joe is speaking to him, but he turns his head just a fraction and those bright eyes reach out to me.

I meet a stare that doesn't make me itch to hurt. He doesn't watch me.

He sees me.

What is he seeing? My long blonde hair covers part of my face. I'm skinnier than I once was. The arms that hang at my sides are only decorated by the small scars from a never-ending stay at Silverwing and my blue-green veins that create paths below my skin.

The very same veins that the nurses use to betray me, pumping me with sedatives to keep me under control.

I wonder if, in my moments of passion, I am a fool.

I should stop wondering. It's as pointless as hoping.

He's still staring at me, all through my inner thinkings. I turn away and continue walking the perimeter of the room, wondering if maybe my reaction has to do with the fact that he looks close to my age. Or how beautifully he wears every second he's ever lived, hunched over a little, lips relaxed into a thin line. He is at ease with his suffering. So at ease, it's as if he's made a coat of it and wears it all his days.

I've never asked anyone why they're in here. And no one's asked me. Not even the somewhat sane nurses. The staff is likely more than knowledgeable on every note in my file and the patrons here are otherwise occupied.

But something about this person and his contradicting looks—soft and sharp all at once—begs for the question to be asked.

One look at him and I don't know if I could ever kill him. *Did my face ever warm like this? Was I ever this curious?*

Before I was locked up in this place, I used to have sex. I used to smile at the boys in my prep school and let them shove their penises inside me. A smile, really, was all it took most times. I liked the way it felt, knowing they were vulnerable in those moments. I'd let them grind against me and I'd watch them as they finished, always knowing exactly what they were thinking.

This is the best feeling in the world.

Was it? Maybe I'd never know how that feels other than in the moments I managed to hurt.

I skirt around the edges of the room as Joe leaves the new cattle member inside with us. He doesn't have the fidgety look most of the new patients have at the idea of being stuck in here.

I admit, on my first day I kept looking at the windows and doors, trying to find the best way to escape while still hoping my sister would show up and take me away from here. After all, it wasn't just *my* fault I wound up here. The phantom-like feel of pain lacing through the seam of the puckered skin of my scar reminds me of that.

But every day that passed was like a fresh blade pushed into my body until I stopped counting the days.

I glance over my shoulder because I swear I can feel someone's stare. Sure enough, those brilliant eyes are on me again.

They don't follow me to keep track of me for his own safety.

They're regarding me with curiosity and they don't blink or hide from me when I meet them.

My skin heats all over again and I look away.

I can't make out his thoughts.

Am I broken?

Have I been broken all along?

8 ABEL

HELL HAS A STAINED TILE CEILING.

There's nothing welcoming about this goddamn place. I start counting the splotches above me.

Pretty soon I'm blinking slower and slower and then I'm not seeing the ceiling anymore.

Before I can sink deep into sleep, I feel my chair jerk and I sit up quickly.

"What the fuck?" I say, not so loud that I scare people but loud enough that the person standing beside me hears.

"They don't like it when we fall asleep."

Her voice is soft, and the violence Dr. Brown warned me about is so far from my mind in that moment. Soft lips and soft words. Even though her eyes seem calculating, looking over me and taking stock of me, they aren't angry, or crazy, even.

"They?"

She sways her head a little toward the nurses' station near the door. They're looking over at us and I wonder what has their attention. They aren't even speaking. Just watching us.

"Are we not allowed to talk to each other?" I glance at her before looking back at them.

"They're just waiting to see how long it takes me to try to hurt you," she says.

I almost laugh but as I look at her, I realize she's serious. Ma would call her crazy. *All this mishegas,* she'd whisper in my ear, beer on her breath. Maybe *mishegas* is what I need because I don't let it stop with that sentence. "Why would you want to do that?"

She stares at me like she's trying to figure out what comes next. I'm eager to see what she decides. Her blonde hair is so long. I want to run my fingers through it, maybe wrap the strands in my fist as I kiss her pink lips. There's something serene about her and I'm thinking maybe she's a contradiction. Violent serenity.

I haven't gotten laid in so long. Girls don't like fucking home-less guys. Is it the fact that my dick hasn't felt anything other than my hand since I can remember that makes me react to her like this?

It's not like I have a ton of options.

But then her eyes squint a little like I'm a puzzle she's trying to piece together and I can't stop staring at her. She took in all of me and now she's trying to put the picture together.

"You keep looking at me and I don't know how to read you."

I draw my brows together. "You say that like it's a bad thing." Who wants to know *everything*? That doesn't sound fun. Fucking stressful, if anything. I can't even handle all of *my* thoughts, most days.

She surprises me by sitting next to me, not close enough to seem intimate but I still take it as a good sign. She tucks her hair behind her ear and those green eyes stare at me like I'm the most important person in the room. She's dazzled by my newness if her eyes tell me anything.

"I think I've been waiting for you," she says.

And I silently vow to never look at her the way Dr. Brown did. I don't even know her fucking name. I'm making promises to a nameless girl at this point. Anything to help the time go by.

If my sentence is anything like today, time will go by quickly.

Welcome to Mishegas Manor, I think to myself as her eyes sparkle with excitement.

"How old are you?" she asks.

She doesn't even know my name. At least, *I* haven't told her my name. "Nineteen now." I remember spending my birthday working and to say it fucking sucked wouldn't do the experience justice at all. If I hadn't been working all damn day, I would've cracked a beer and had a cheap meal somewhere before passing out in my car. Still, it would've been a day full of choices I decided to make as opposed to hearing my boss screaming at me.

"I want to guess your name but I don't think I'd get it," she says. "You don't look like you have a normal name." The hair that slid from behind her ear is tucked right back there again. "I'll be a little disappointed if your name isn't special."

"Why?" I ask. *Are we flirting? In a mental institution? Is this really happening?* I smile because fuck it. There wasn't anything like her outside of this place.

"You don't look like everyone else. So how could you have a name like everyone else?"

Her eyes aren't losing their sparkle and I find myself trying to come up with something flirty to say as quickly as I can. But screw that. I want to take my time and say shit I've thoroughly thought out. She waits as I think of the best way to answer her.

"Well, what's your name?" I ask, mostly because I really want to know and I can't think of anything better than that. My game is *way* off.

"Rose."

Holy shit, her name is perfect. I feel like I should be reciting some fucking Shakespeare quote when she says it. And now it's my turn to speak. "Rose." I say her name, hoping it sticks in some part of my brain. The part that knows about destiny and all that shit because sitting next to her feels like I'm not in a crazy house. It feels like we're two normal people, just talking.

Until some lady screams across the room and I jerk out of my chair to see what's wrong.

Rose makes a sound of stifled amusement and grabs my hand to pull me back into my seat. One touch and I'm staring at the way her hand feels in mine.

When she sees me notice the contact, she pulls her hand away. *Does she think I didn't like it?*

"Tell me your name," she says when my ass hits the chair.

It's quiet but it's a command. I don't mind it. These people watch her like her touch hurts but I've only witnessed the softness of it. I already want more.

"Abel. Like Cain and Abel. Sommerfeldt. Like...I don't know." I shrug one shoulder and she smiles. I wish there was a polite way to ask her to touch me again without sounding like a fucking weirdo. But, I mean, I'm in the right place to act a little fucking weirdo.

"For once, I'm not disappointed," she whispers.

I don't know if I was supposed to hear it, but I'm glad I did. I look back at the nurses and they are whispering amongst each other as they continue to stare at us. "Are they afraid of you or something?"

Some of the nurses are walking around the room, engaging with a few of the other patients. But they don't come near us. They stare, they talk, but they don't approach.

"I've been here too long to care." Those eyes don't take a break from their direct stare. They catch every move I make.

"How long have you been here?" Before I can wonder if it was wrong of me to ask that, she offers her answer easily.

"Nearly three years."

Mishigas, mishigas, mishigas, my ma's voice is warning me.

Three years in here and everyone is afraid of her. I should stop flirting with her. I should stop imagining how good it would feel to fuck her. I should stop wondering what her lips taste like and if she would open like a rose if I spread her legs—soft pink petals, ripe for plucking.

I should.
I should.
I should.
But I don't.
I've done worse things than this.
What's the worst that could happen?

9 ROSE

His name is Abel Sommerfeldt and he doesn't belong here. He's been here a few days, and these are the things I know: he is firmly rooted in his reality and when he smiles, he isn't tormented. He smiles often when I'm around. When he doesn't know I'm looking, his lips are in that resting line, like he's thinking about things that are boring to him but the line between his eyebrows indicate these thoughts could be troublesome to others.

I'm likely reaching because I have nothing but time to ponder all the things he could be thinking of.

He is already an array of colors on the blandness that has become my life here.

We're waiting in line for breakfast and I try not to stare at him. His hair is disheveled, but it doesn't make him any less attractive to me. It's a little unfair, how sharp his jaw is and how blue his eyes are. I wonder whose doing that was. His mother? His father?

I want to laugh at myself. The same girl—woman now—who didn't care to know anything about anyone else in here is filling her head with questions to fire at this person as soon as we sit.

That's our routine now, I think.

We sit to eat, and I ask him all the questions I can think of. My questions don't bother him, if his smile is any indication. He doesn't look away, he doesn't hide himself from me. He does not fear me and that does not anger me.

One time he bumped me a little with his shoulder. Had it been anyone else, I would've reacted a little differently.

Very differently, I correct myself as he reaches for his plastic spoon and starts eating.

I ask him these questions because I'm trying to figure out what makes him safe from me. "Your blue eyes. Did you get them from your mother or father?"

He swallows a spoonful of his own watery oatmeal and chuckles a little, like he's privy to a joke that I'm unaware of.

An agitated curiosity unfurls deep in my belly. I crave that knowledge, to know what causes his dry pleasure to escape from his body in such a thoughtless way.

"Definitely not my ma," he says.

"Why the laugh?" I haven't even touched my food yet and I ignore everyone else around us.

"It's just that my ma hated my eyes. She kinda thought Jewish people shouldn't have blue eyes. Even tried to carve a swastika in my skin 'cause I didn't have brown eyes like her."

Words said so casually lance through this heart that I always thought would never work that way. I squeeze my fists so hard in my lap that I can feel my nails digging into my palm. If this woman was in front of me, I'd tear her apart with my bare hands. "But she did sleep with your blue-eyed father to create you, yes?" I ask after a moment, trying to sound merely curious. No Mr. Hyde in sight. I am Dr. Jekyll for this man; the best Bruce Banner there ever was.

"That's where it gets a little tricky. The man she claimed is my father doesn't have blue eyes either. And I guess he wasn't happy about the timing of her pregnancy. Always saying I'm not his fucking kid." He shrugs before taking another bite.

"So you don't know who your father is?"

He licks the corners of his lips. "I guess not. I always thought it was him but maybe that's why my ma had it so hard after me, you know? Maybe it's because she was a little lost and I remind her of that. Drove her to drink. I know she was engaged to my dad before, but they never got married. And I guess he ended up marrying someone else."

He talks about her in past tense, as if she somehow stopped existing; only residing in his memories. "How did she die?" I ask.

He shrugs again but opens his mouth to speak.

Did her death make him sad? Did he cry?

"One night she got shitfaced and just didn't wake up."

"How old were you?"

He shifts in his seat, but the way his body is facing me with his eyes focused on me, clear as a summer sky, I don't get the feeling that he's uncomfortable.

"Fourteen."

I push my oatmeal around the bowl. I was still free when I was fourteen. I hadn't yet become a prisoner. Sometimes I wish I could go back and change some things; change how trusting and naïve and carefree I was.

Then I remember that I can't do that and even if I *could*, some people just deserve to hurt the way I'd delivered it. Some people just deserve to bleed and cry and even die.

But not Abel.

Abel deserves more.

He does not belong here.

"What's your favorite part about being here, Rose?"

I lift a brow and tilt my head a little. As soon as he sees my reaction, he smiles. I want to reach out and put it in my pocket for the days I'm in solitary and counting.

It would make me forget to count.

He has no fat on his face to soften his features. When he smiles, what might've been dimples are just lines framing his lips. The action looks like he's thinking ominous thoughts as opposed to pleasurable ones. Maybe, for him, it's one and the same. But one glance at the warmth in his eyes tells me he's kind.

"I'm serious," he says. "We're already fucking here. May as well talk about the things we like."

I shove my tray away from me and he picks up my spoon and starts eating my breakfast. I press my palms together to keep my hands from reaching to touch him in a way no one here would recognize. Certainly not from me, anyway. "Well, I suppose I'm happy that I don't have to brush my hair."

"I'm happy I don't have to worry about how I'll eat," he says.

That one makes me pause but because this is a game, I don't dwell too much on his answer, even if it makes me hurt for him. The kind I'd have to hurt the whole world to fix. "I'm happy I don't have to attend my mother's terrible luncheons." I can still feel the hot curling wand as I sat unmoving to have my hair neat and styled to perfection.

"I'm happy...that I..." he taps his finger to his full lower lip, "don't have to watch the news and hear about how terrible the world is."

"I'm happy people don't bother me."

"Even if it's out of fear?" he asks.

I press my lips together for a moment to keep from telling him that I'd bitten a nurse. I prefer fear to any other mockery of respect. "They should be afraid of me."

Something else sits on my tongue and he looks at me like he can taste the possibility of the nectar in what I'm wanting to say next.

And so, because I decide nerves are for the weak, I give him something I didn't know I had. *Softness.* "I think, perhaps, you're the only person who shouldn't be."

His smile is so wide and open, looking strange on that face that's entirely too harsh for his spirit. "And why is that?"

Because hurting you might hurt me, too.

I want to shake the impossible thought away, but I acknowledge the truth to it instead. It's entirely too obvious to me.

What's obvious to you may be foreign to someone else, I remind myself. Joe told me a variation of that during our last session and I ignored it until this moment.

"Because I'd miss your company too much if I killed you," I say. "I don't want you to be afraid of me and I don't want to be afraid of my anger when I'm with you."

He puffs his lips out, making them look fuller than they already are, his cheeks hollowing for a moment. "Sounds good."

That's all it takes for me to relax. "How are you liking Joe?" I ask Abel and his energy shifts, his smile evaporating the more he absorbs my question, like remembering where we are takes away what momentary distractions we allow ourselves.

He runs his fingers through his hair, scissoring the strands as if their existence annoys him. "Something about him bothers me."

Abel's age shows in his annoyance. He pouts for a moment, his eyes not on me as he tries in vain to figure out what it is about the man in question that vexes him so.

My mother would hate the way he expresses himself, dismissing him as unintelligent. My mother is *no* genius. I know better. "He's a ghost of a man," I say clearly, for anyone to overhear. "Or under a ventriloquist's control."

"It's more than that." He leans forward. "He just gives off such a weird vibe."

"I don't see any radioactive spiders hanging around, Peter Parker," I tell him, and he snorts out a laugh, snagging the attention of several other members of the cattle.

Do I joke like this? Is this something I do now?

He shakes his head and I continue.

"You'll get used to him."

"I think that's what freaks me out. I don't wanna get used to him. I wanna go home."

For once, I'm at a loss for words.

I've nearly run out of hope for a future like one Abel hints at. Joe smothers it with every reminder.

I don't own you. You own yourself. Your actions are to blame for the life you're now living.

I hate the smugness that constantly coats his easygoing smile.

Abel, however, is still coming to terms with his punishment.

My obsession with retaliation is forcing the question from my thoughts and into the air through my lips. "Why are you here?" It's the question I've wanted to ask since the day I saw him falling asleep in his chair. I saved that question just for him. He's the only one whose history I want to know.

He isn't like anyone here. Is unlike anyone I'd ever met.

He is the sun peeking between the dreary clouds and I am the girl wanting to sing. *You are my sunshine…*

Abel makes me a giddy fool.

"I…I don't remember it all."

I don't know this Abel; timid and unsure. He reaches under the table to wipe his palms on his shapeless pants and I take one of them in mine.

Those bright eyes flicker to me, a question in them.

The genius in me draws a blank.

Perhaps…can I trust you? What will you think of me?

I pause.

Tell him why you're here, I tell myself. But he speaks again before I can offer to ruin his image of me with only a few words.

"I tried to jump off the twenty-second story of a building. At first, no one noticed. Apparently, I'd been there for hours and, I don't know why, Rose. I don't know what happened. It's like I was fucking dreaming."

One shaky inhale, one hand squeezing mine, and he continues.

"It's so fucking real to be reminded that no one cares. Because I'm nobody."

He doesn't pick his head back up until the last few words fall out and they punch me in the chest.

Because I'm nobody.

I've always felt like the center of the world, even in here.

"You don't remember wanting to jump?"

He's shaking his head. His hands rub over his jaw and then his lips. "Homeless, living out of my car, working whatever odd job I could find, my life was already fucked up. I had every reason to want to jump. But, it's not something I could ever see myself doing. I just had no clue what the fuck was going on. Not until I was down and saw myself on the goddamn news."

Homeless.

Something else I wouldn't know about. My parents had entirely too much money to know what to do with, sending me to the best private schools and buying my sister her own horse. We had vacation homes and nice, shiny cars.

Even now, I'm being taken care of. Even if it's of little to no service, unlike the lifestyle I'm used to.

Money is not begot by some sort of god. No one is lined up based on their level of *special* and handed a thick wad of cash to rule the world with. Any one person can have a large amount of money—even the utterly vile.

Money can only mask the truth.

The truth is, we're all a little unstable. We all have that bit of monster in us, a Mr. Hyde. Most relate this to the angel on one shoulder and the devil on the other.

I don't because if I did, there'd only be one and the devil would be so large, I'd need to have him hooked to a leash instead of perched on my shoulder.

He'd have murdered the angel by now.

I let go of Abel's hand and set it on the table, but he follows my movement and grips my fingers before they have the chance to hit the tabletop, like we aren't being watched.

From the nurses' station, I hear someone shout, "No touching!"

He jerks his hand away and I want to find the person that said that and squeeze their neck until they stop talking and—by default —breathing.

"You're a good friend, Rose," he whispers with a small smile. The smile he usually wears is sweeter and surer than the one he offers now.

Still, I bask under it, like sunshine on my pale skin.

You are my sunshine...

Then he's looking down at his fingernails and the moment is gone. I look over at the nurses' station and glare at them.

"Don't," Abel says.

And I flinch before facing him again.

"I shouldn't touch you," he says.

"You shouldn't?" I ask, because I don't know that I'll ever be fluent in Abel Sommerfeldt. My genius doesn't work with him.

He's shaking his head. "Maybe if we weren't in this shit hole..."

"Do you think we'd be friends if we weren't here?" He doesn't make me feel stupid for not knowing who he is. He often looks at me like I surprise him but he's a shock to what I find "normal" since coming to Silverwing.

"You wouldn't look twice at someone like me. So, no."

I push my hair from my face and my chair screeches a little as I turn to face him completely. "I'm a few things. Self-centered, abrasive, violent, impossible to tame, quite possibly abnormal. If you ask Joe, he'd be more than willing to add to it, but I know 'snob' isn't on that list, even if I was raised by one." I would look once, twice, a hundred times. He's a walking contradiction: a man that looks like he's capable of hurting the world but only offering me friendship while sharing peaceful silence with everyone else. The only reason everyone avoids him is because he's with me the majority of the time. "I know I belong here. But you don't."

He smiles.

This one makes me bite the inside of my cheek.

"You definitely don't belong here," he says. "You belong in a penthouse with a rich boyfriend."

"You can't wish that boring life on me, Abel." I nearly shudder at the picture he painted. I've done the rich boys. They're all small penises, big wallets, and boring conversation. Something tells me Abel isn't *anything* like them.

My parents were part of that "perfect life" Abel envisions. They spent more time fighting—with their fists and words—and then smiling perfectly in their pictures than being happy.

"Then tell me, where would you be?"

I take a moment because I want to make sure I say this right, if I bother to say it at all. "Today, my answer is anywhere with you." It's probably the sweetest thing I've ever said to a person and it drips from my tongue easily the way the truth often does.

"Yeah?" He clasps his hands together.

If I could read him, maybe I'd know if it's because he's trying hard to keep his hands to himself.

"Definitely. Everyone else treats me like I'm a wild animal."

I am wild and I am violent but I am falling at your feet, wanting to show you my affections in blood.

I've known him for as long as it takes some food to expire. Still, I offer my round edges to him almost thoughtlessly.

"Nah. Just a rose with a few thorns." He leans back in his chair, his hands in his lap. "Fuck 'em."

I smile and it's the first time I've smiled all day.

He doesn't belong here but while he is, I will pretend he's mine.

10 ABEL

"I UNDERSTAND YOU'VE BEEN SPENDING A LOT OF TIME with Rosamunde."

I've only just sat down when Dr. Brown says this, and I have no fucking idea what he's talking about.

"Rose," he says.

Realization dawns. Her full name is Rosamunde. It kinda puts the fact that I don't know much about her in perspective. I nod but don't speak because as far as I'm concerned, as long as we aren't killing each other, it's none of his damn business.

"I just want to make several points before I get on with our session."

I gesture with my hand for him to continue. It's not like I can just get up and walk out. I need this asshole in order to get the hell out of here. He removes his reading glasses and stares at me without blinking.

It's like he can see inside my goddamn head, all the versions of me who live in there.

And that other extra tenant.

Dirty goy, I could hear my ma announce.

"I don't have to remind you that this isn't a matchmaking

service. This is a respected mental institute where you're receiving treatment for your mental instability."

This is where I want to call him out on his bullshit. This *is* fucking bullshit. We both know I shouldn't be here. Ma would tell him to eat shit and die, spitting at his feet.

"*But,*" he says, before I can interrupt, "if we take that completely out of the equation and just factor Ms. Montgomery into this, it would be doomed from the start. Any sort of romance, I mean."

Yeah, man. I'm not fucking stupid.

Still sucks balls to hear.

Still doesn't change the tightness in my chest, knowing that this asshole is telling me to stay away from her.

"You are somewhat defiant. It's the young man in you. You've lived on your own for quite some time and you think you know what's best for you. This isn't something I find to be too troubling. Annoying, certainly. But you aren't detrimental in your defiance." He puts his glasses back on and sits back in his squeaky leather chair.

My middle finger is itching to be shoved in this guy's face over calling me annoying. Pretty sure this isn't professional. Pretty sure he shouldn't be talking to me about Rose at all since that violates… some shit. A right I know she has.

"I can't say the same thing for Rose. She has a complete disregard for authority to the point of sheer aggression. She is a hazard to all and it's unlikely that any real relationship will be lasting."

I blink a few times because what the fuck does this even mean for me? I guess he takes my silence as permission to continue.

"She has violent outbursts. Someone interrupted her conversation with another patient and she stabbed her in the arm with a pen. She's volatile and erratic. Her anger knows no bounds and even the staff have been subjected to her outbursts. On one of her birthdays, she nearly bit off a nurse's ear after attacking one of our male patients because he sneezed on her. So, you see, whatever you're building with her can easily sour. And you'd never see it coming, Mr. Sommerfeldt."

"Rose and I are just friends. And as far she goes, why not have a little faith? Maybe this friendship will help her." While we *are* just friends, it feels wrong to paint it as if I don't want her. I wanted her from the moment I saw her and it sounds fucking idiotic but I'll probably want her long after I leave here. There's something about her that draws me in.

She isn't like any other girl, that's for sure. But she has a certain substance and class to her. The way she talks, even the way she walks, like she's walking to somewhere of importance in some beautiful gown, instead of in these shitty hallways with cheap fucking pajamas on.

She owns this mysterious quality she has and I want nothing more than to figure her out. To know her intimately.

But I can't even hold her fucking hand here.

"I admire your optimism, Abel, but she's been my patient for three years. While I've never seen her react to anyone the way she has to you, at some point, you will leave our program. I have faith that you'll move on to better things. But this is Rose's home. And as long as she shows no improvement, this will remain her home."

Part of me completely rejects the idea of Rose staying here forever. She should be with the rest of the world, watching movies, listening to music, and being as fucking beautiful as she is. "Does she know this?"

"I've been explaining this to her. Certainly, that she's to blame for her current living situation. It's my hope that this will reroute her way of thinking, get her to take responsibility for her actions, and push her toward better behavior and more self-control. It's strange because no matter the medication, she doesn't respond."

I remain stoic because I don't want to give away the fact that I know she doesn't take her medication—and neither do I, for that matter. She's shared all her tips for survival in Purgatory with me and I'll take them to the grave before I ever let them turn Rose into a walking corpse like the rest of these people.

"I typically don't like to talk about patients with other patients, but I figured you should know this, going in."

I don't ask him what got her here because I want her to tell me. She deserves to be the only person to tell me, just as I was the only person to tell her what I know about how the hell I got stuck here.

There's just some shit you gotta hear from the horse's mouth.

I'm still gutted by the idea of Rose living and dying here. She's only nineteen. She hasn't had a legal drink, will never get married and have children. What kind of bullshit is this?

What the hell did she do?

Dr. Brown asks me something, pulling me from my thoughts and I grimace at the fact that we still have an hour left to talk about me and my fucking feelings.

Great.

"They finally faxed over Dr. Levine's notes. She suggests you might've had a bit of a schizophrenic episode, for lack of better terms."

"Oh?" I sit back and cross my ankle over my knee. These tighty whities are so damn uncomfortable, but I'm not about to let this man know while he sits here and tries to dissect me. *Good luck, motherfucker.*

"She also seems to think this is something you may be susceptible to again, should you be in an extremely stressful environment."

My ankle starts to shake, and his eyes follow the movement for a moment.

"Does any of this sound feasible, Abel?"

My shrug is all he gets.

"I mean, her notes are pretty thorough for only having sat with you for a little over an hour. She mentions homelessness, a situation that could certainly be considered high-stress. There are also some physical indications you've given. A lack of eye contact, on any one thing or even on her, jumpiness," he says, shuffling between papers as he adjusts his glasses and squints, "suggesting that you may believe there is another person or entity in the room with the two of you."

"Now, I never said that, Dr. Brown," I tell him as I set both feet on the ground and lean forward. "I never said any of that shit."

He places his hands up, as if we've agreed on some sort of white flag.

"Schizophrenic? You guys are really taking this shit that far?"

"Abel, I just want to know what's going on. And I need you to be honest with me if you want to get out of here. Many people go on to live almost-normal lives with schizophrenia. I don't want you to see this as the beginning of the end but the beginning of you getting the help you need to get healthy again, okay?"

My nod is apparently all this fucking guy needs to continue as I stare out the window, wishing I could be out there, feeling anything other the heat of my ma's stare at my back.

"Tell me about your mother, Abel."

11 ROSE

My twentieth birthday is a month away. I think of the promise I made myself after spending days in solitary.

But that was before Abel.

It doesn't matter.

It isn't like Abel can save me from this place. He will survive in spite of his stay and I will become every type of monster they can think of before I die here. Alone.

And he will forget about me.

And I will be stuck here. I will die alone, and no one will visit my grave because I will not have had a life filled with people who want to celebrate me once I've gone.

The thoughts pound on in my head as I head toward the rec room, anxious to see Abel. I don't think about these things around him and it's so wonderful to get out of my head sometimes.

The genius eats me alive some days.

When I look up, I see him just inside, and I take advantage of the fact that he hasn't seen me yet.

He's looking down at his fingers, picking at a hangnail or something, but I notice the way his lips are settled. They aren't in their typical relaxed state; they tip down even a fraction and I'm wondering why. He still doesn't see me, so I just stand there and stare. He's done with his fingernails and moves on to his uniform, picking at the small pieces of fuzz and dirt that he's somehow managed to pick up.

I wonder how we will greet each other today. *Will he still make me smile? Will he meet my violence? Will I destroy our friendship?*

I'm asking myself these questions when he looks up at me. And then the questions are silenced as he smiles slowly and waves. I swear, each smile is better than its predecessor. *How is that possible?*

In my world, people are flat and lifeless and only ever entertaining when they're reacting to pain until they are quite literally lifeless.

And then I met Abel and he made me question myself.

More than that, he makes me want to believe in something. Destiny and fate are for the weak, ideas I've never subscribed to. I don't want to believe that there's a path for every person because I'd have to face the idea of not being on mine. I've veered off somewhere and I don't know that I can ever get back on.

But if I did believe in these frivolities, I'd likely believe that Abel has a sprinkle of that magic in him. That he exists, excites me. That he smiles, sweetens me. And that he calls me, calms me.

I head toward him, and his smile is still in place.

"You were looking awful thoughtful over there, Rose," he says.

"One could say the same about you, Mr. Sommerfeldt."

He pinches his chin as I sit beside him. "Your full name," he says. "What is it?"

Strange that I feel like I've known him for a long time, but he doesn't even know my full name. I spend so much time asking *him* questions. "Rosamunde Montgomery. But I prefer Rose."

"Not Rosa?" he asks with a playful grin.

I shake my head. "Just Rose."

"Well, *Just Rose,* should we talk about the shit we hate about this place today?"

I watch as his hands slide against the table top until they're a few inches from my crossed arms. He spreads his fingers and I smile. "Is that how you're feeling, today? We'll be here forever."

"Fuck it, I'll start." He pulls his hands back toward himself and crosses his arms as well. "I hate that I have to wear these tighty whities they gave me. My junk isn't exactly loving the fact that they're a little too fucking small."

I giggle, and it feels as foreign as it sounds. Strange enough that the already quiet room has turned silent. I glance around the room and the nurses' eyes are all wide with shock. "I hate that people always *stare*," I say loudly enough so they can hear me.

Abel just smiles and sits up. "I hate that I can't listen to music."

I nod in agreement. Anything is better than the silence and the screams. "I hate that I've spent three birthdays here. And I hate that I never want to spend another here."

"That was two. Don't get greedy, Rose." He shakes his finger at me. "Think you'll be out by your next birthday?"

I shake my head, slowly, and hold his stare. "It's next month."

His lips part as he stares at me, like he's trying to understand how that must feel for me. Even *if* I could transfer emotions, I wouldn't do it to him. Not to someone I thoroughly enjoy.

"One day you'll be able to spend your birthday with the rest of the world. And I'll be right next to you, helping you get fucking wasted."

He talks about it like it can happen for me and I love that more than anything I can think of. Even more than envisioning the way I'd kill everyone on my mental hit list.

"I hate that it took you so long to get here," I whisper. The words are clear but quietly so, thanks to my practice in speaking in hushed tones with him.

"I hate that I never knew you were here, waiting."

One of his hands slides toward the middle up the table, palm up. I stare at it for a moment. "I hate that this it for us."

"I hate that you think that," he counters.

"I love that you think there could be...*more*." I want to cover my eyes because, the way I feel, they're full of emotions I can't quite understand. And Abel might be fluent in me. But I hardly blink, let alone look away.

"I hate that I'm scared to think of a future where you and I aren't a possibility."

My lips twitch. *With sadness at his words or happiness at the emotions behind them?* "I hate solitary. I hate that I count just so I have something to focus on. I hate that they know how much I hate it and they use it against me. Once I stop counting, it's like they win because I start to lose myself."

I press my palms together. I don't pray. Any higher power surely curses my existence. And, because I have nothing to pray to, I share my secret with Abel.

"I hate that I promised I'd kill myself before I spend another birthday here. I hate that I still want to do it."

His next exhale is shaky, and he moves his other hand toward me before squeezing them into fists and pressing them into the table top. "I hate that I can't hug you." It's the quietest his words have ever been.

I press the heels of my palms into my thighs, not really sure how to respond. It isn't a terrible feeling, being rendered speechless. There's something to be said for it, under the right circumstances. The words that hang between us are decorated with those unrecognizable emotions.

He makes it so easy to forget that I'm in captivity. We're both in our own cages only he's reaching for me like we can somehow live like this.

But he won't always be here.

And once he's gone...

The girl who loves being left alone is now afraid of the idea of it.

It only took the right person, a few hundred questions, and a couple of weeks for it to happen.

12 ABEL

"WHAT ARE YOU THINKING ABOUT, ABEL?"

Fuck, I can tell he's trying to be nice, but all Dr. Brown succeeds in doing is making me feel fucking cornered.

"That I cannot *breathe* in this goddamn place," I grit out, ready to punch a wall or pick up something and throw it, just so *I'm* not the broken thing in this motherfucking room.

My eyes open when I hear his sigh.

He takes his glasses off and pinches the bridge of his nose. "Listen, I don't think you're so far gone. If I'm being completely honest here, I don't think you belong here. But being uncooperative, being a person with less than a desirable income. Essentially, being a person without the proper resources to help yourself has landed you here. But I promise you, I will do all I can..."

My dry chuckle has him stopping. "You can't even save the people who've been here for years."

He shakes his head. "I'm not sure if you're aware, but this isn't exactly the place people go to be rehabilitated." He puts his glasses back on and writes something down in his notebook. "But you're not like them."

The breath on my neck tells me otherwise and I remind myself...*she isn't here. She isn't here and she can't hurt me anymore.*

She isn't in control. She's fucking dead and I will spend the rest of my days ignoring her, pretending I don't see her, so she'll die in my head, too.

"How about we take a little field trip, huh?"

He must see the surprise on my face because he laughs.

"I think it'd do us both some good to be around people a little more...settled."

"What? Nurses not keeping you happy with their sparkling personalities?" I ask.

Dr. Brown snorts and I don't know where the fuck this is all coming from but I'm all right with seeing him a little less like a nerdy robot. He might actually be cool.

"Some of these nurses shouldn't be paid to be here," he says, under his breath but I can still hear every word.

I don't laugh, though. I don't want to react and break whatever good mood he's in as he heads to the door, opens it, and looks out.

"You don't have to sneak out, man," I say.

"You're right. I don't." He turns back and waves me toward him. "But you do."

I don't bother looking around as we head out the door, the good doctor behind me, telling me where to go.

"Turn away, please," he says once we reach a door that requires a code to enter.

I hear a beep and then we're walking down a few flights. I figure there's another code to leave the building, but no. A simple push of the door with the exit sign over it and we're outside. The sun is beating down on me and I have to shut my eyes, it's so fucking bright.

It's even bright there, behind my lids, so I see the flesh shade of my lids until I squeeze my eyes tighter.

I wish for blonde locks and her small smiles.

I want to know what she looks like under the golden sun.

"You don't have to keep your eyes closed, Abel," I hear Dr. Brown say.

His words sound a little strange, like he has something in his mouth. When I open my eyes, I see he's lighting a cigarette.

"What the hell, Dr. Brown?"

"Would you like one?"

But he hands his over and pulls out a new one before I can answer. And I'm smoking outside with this man I'm probably supposed to fucking hate.

He's making it really hard not to.

"I hope you can keep a secret," he says, his eyes on the sky, squinting.

I don't bother responding.

No need to disappoint anyone else.

13 ROSE

"HOW ARE WE TODAY, ROSE?"

Here he goes with the dreaded *we* again. *"I'm* fine. How are you, Joe?"

I've been in this room enough times that I could maneuver blindly without bumping into anything. Maybe Joe doesn't see our relationship as a window, but I do. I know he can see me, but does he realize I can see him as well?

"As good as always," he answers easily but he fidgets with his glasses in a way that I don't usually see.

"Are you sure?"

He drops his hand, clears his throat, and nods. "Quite sure. But I want to discuss something with you."

"Isn't that why we're here? All I've been doing for the past three years is discussing things with you, Joe. The day you bring me in here to play hopscotch will be the day I'm genuinely at a loss for words."

He cracks a small smile but it's fleeting.

Nothing at all what Abel offers.

"What is it?" I whisper the question, afraid of this man who holds my fate in his hands. I hate it. I hate how itchy it feels to not be the master of my life. No matter what he says, I'm his and no one cares.

"I just want to warn you about your new friendship…"

My brows are drawn by the end of his sentence. "Why? I haven't done anything to him or anyone else. He seems to be *helping* me, if anything." I grit my teeth. I don't want to say more and risk Joe seeing the intensity of my feelings.

"Believe me when I say I have your best interests at heart. But I want to put things in perspective for you, Rosamunde."

I clench my fist at my full name and he takes off his glasses.

"In all the time you've been here, your progress has been minimal. You refuse to accept treatment while Abel readily accepts his. Abel is already leaps and bounds ahead of you on the road to recovery."

"That's because there's nothing *wrong* with Abel," I cry out and stand.

Joe flinches and I hate it more than I ever thought I would.

I sit back down.

"I want to make sure you don't get so attached that when he leaves you lash out."

When he leaves…when he leaves…

Those aren't words I want to hear right now.

"It isn't like he's leaving tomorrow, Joe." I cross my arms and sit back in my chair.

"True, yes. But I'm saying this now, in the beginning. Listen to me…"

"I was never any good at listening." I stand and move toward the door, but I know he has to agree to end the session before our time is up. If I walk out, I could face time in solitary. I clench my jaw for a moment before turning back to look at him. "May I leave?"

He stares at me as I squeeze the doorknob. When he waves his hand, I rush out of the room.

I don't bother to shut the door behind me for the next cattle member that has to spend an hour with him.

14 ABEL

ROSE IS STILL IN WITH DR. BROWN. I KEEP GLANCING toward the door because I'm fidgety and I don't know why. I have no idea what the fuck is up with me, but I can't sit still. Maybe it's because she told me was suicidal and I figure if I have my eye on her or if she's with Dr. Brown, she's okay.

I've never cared about someone as much as I care about her. Not even my ma. I should be ashamed of that. After the things she'd done to me, I couldn't bring myself to care as much about her as I should've.

I didn't even cry when she died.

Maybe my fucking heart has been empty all along and because of it, it's Rose's for the taking. The entire damn thing.

I should feel cornered and screwed and all those things guys usually feel when faced with something *huge*, but I refuse to. I've come too far to let myself back out just because I'm being a pussy. No way.

This *shlimazel* has finally got a bit of luck. Typically, an unlucky bastard, I'm waiting for the other shoe to drop. And I have a feeling that shit's going to make a fucking racket when it does.

Where I'm seated, I can see Rose head down the hall toward the rec room, her blonde hair flowing freely as she walks. She moves slowly like she's got all the time in the world and she doesn't see me yet so I look at her the way I rarely ever can because I don't want to intimidate her. She's comfortable staring and asking questions and I don't want to fuck that up just because I'm selfish. Sure, we need each other in this weird way that gives us some fucked up version of hope. Or happiness. But she needs me more.

I love the way her arms swing in time with her steps. The movement makes her look happy and I know it's fucking strange to think but I just want her to be happy. Every day. Even if just for a moment.

If I can make her happy, maybe she'll change.

And maybe I won't have to leave her behind one day.

I'm in my head so fucking deep that when a man accidentally bumps into her as he makes his way around her toward the rec room, I'm not a hundred percent focused on her. A split second is all it takes.

A split fucking second and I can see the change in her.

I am witnessing what everyone is afraid of as her face contorts in anger. She reaches for the back of the man's top and I'm out of my chair, rushing toward the now scrapping pair. As I get closer, I see he's on his stomach and she's pushing his face into the ground. The blood is already leaking from his nose when I feel someone push me aside.

"Rose!"

At the sound of my shout, she looks up. Right at me. It's like I snapped her out of a fucking trance. She almost *smiles*.

I push the nurse aside and run faster, pulling her into my arms. *I'm finally holding her,* I think as I feel her tremble. "It's okay." I press my cheek into her hair before I'm yanked away.

The nurses grab her roughly and I grab one of them and push him into the wall. The female nurse that's still holding Rose's arm looks at me with wide eyes. Rose breaks away and runs toward me. I've just got her hand in mine when I feel a force tackle me to the ground. The nurse I'd pushed into the wall is sitting on top of me and I can hear Rose's screams. More nurses have made their way to us.

"It's okay," I yell as I struggle against him. "Don't worry about me, Rose."

Her screams start losing force and I turn my head in time to see that they've stuck her with the poison she hates. She fights against it, hiccupping over her anxiety, tears sliding down the side of her face. I'm silent, watching her through her pain and it makes me want to punch my fist through this asshole's chest.

She's still hiccupping and trying to catch her breath when she turns her face to the side to see mine.

"It's okay," I whisper. "It's okay."

She nods, her blinks becoming slower and slower.

And I feel the prick of a needle on the inside of my elbow. "It's okay," I keep saying, even as it gets harder to speak.

It's not okay, Abel, I think to myself as the world goes black.

15 ROSE

I'M BACK IN CAPTIVITY BUT THIS TIME, I SCREAM. I scream and fight and act like the wild animal they've made me become. I bite and snarl and when I've lost my voice, I whisper Abel's name.

And I wonder if I'm a genius or simply a madwoman.

I have hours to wonder if he's okay and if he's afraid of me now.

If I ever uttered a prayer, it'd be for Abel to never be afraid of me.

He is everything good and I scratch at the walls until my fingers bleed because I want that goodness back.

I never cried before. I never screamed. I only ever counted. But I never had anything to lose before. Things are different now.

In my madness, I am desperate. In my infatuation, I am violent for Abel.

Set me free, set me free, I begin to chant to no one. My voice is gone but I am still full of fire even if my hands are bloodied and my eyes sting from my tears and my head pounds from my screaming.

I am full of fire and rage and I will not stop until I'm back with him.

16 ABEL

THERE ARE PEOPLE TALKING AROUND ME AND I FIGHT
the urge to tell them to shut the fuck up. I open my eyes when I
remember why I'm even asleep to begin with. It doesn't feel like
I'm waking up from a nap. My tongue feels heavy and dry in my
mouth and my arms aren't fucking moving.

When I look over, I realize it's because I'm fucking *strapped to
the bed*.

What in the fuck?

Okay, come on. I didn't even do anything.

Wait. I tackled a nurse.

But that isn't even a big fucking *deal*.

Before I can argue it in my mind, I hear Dr. Brown's voice.

"Ah, you're awake, Mr. Sommerfeldt."

So, we're back to Mr. Sommerfeldt.

I hear someone screaming and I wonder. I jerk my arms, hard,
but they don't move. "Rose," I say but her name is slurred.

Dr. Brown clicks his pen. "Don't worry about her. I'm here to
talk about you."

Another scream. Another jerk. Another click.

"Where is she?"

He doesn't answer, only adjusts his glasses and sets his clip-board and pen down. Then he pulls up a chair like we're old fucking pals or something. "She's *fine*, Abel. But, I'm wondering how you're feeling, now that you've seen what she's capable of. Do you think this is something you can just overcome?"

So that's what this is? He's come to thumb his nose in my fucking face like some goody two-shoes. *What a prick.* "I told you. We're just friends."

No more cigarettes or secrets, I guess.

"Yes, well I just want you to know what you're getting into. You have a future beyond this, Abel. Don't jeopardize it over her."

"If I say okay will you let me go?"

"Only if you promise not to go looking for Ms. Montgomery."

I nod.

He squints his eyes for a moment before nodding. "Very well. I like you, Abel. I don't want this for you. Next time, I suggest you let my staff do their jobs."

Several hours later, I'm escorted to my room. Everything feels stiff and I want to crawl out of my fucking skin.

I have no idea where Rose is. *Is she in her bed? Is she in solitary? Is she in a bed like I was in earlier?*

I get up and walk as quietly as I can toward my door. I don't know that I can even go down to solitary without a passcode or something but I can at least walk past her room. There's a nurse making rounds at the end of the hall and I rush toward her room, holding my breath because I don't want to make noise and because I don't know what I'll do if she's not in there.

I near her door and I can't even fucking look. I have to pace for a second and before I lose my nerve, I peek into the small window on her door.

When I see her empty bed, I try not to make a sound but it's really fucking hard because I know what solitary does to her.

I know that she counts at first to keep her calm. But when she stops counting, that's when she starts to lose it.

It's been too long.

She's not counting and I'm not sure what I'm gonna do but I need to get us the fuck out of Silverwing.

I didn't understand why Rose wanted to end her beautiful fucking life, but I get it now.

Silverwing is killing her the longer she stays. So, either she does the job or this fucking place does it for her.

17 ROSE

I'M NOT SORRY THAT THE FIRST TIME JOE CAME IN HERE, I lunged at him. I'm in a straitjacket now and I'm still not sorry.

He's talking but I refuse to acknowledge him. If he didn't want my violence, he shouldn't have taken me from Abel.

If he didn't want my violence, he'd get my silence instead.

"Mr. Sommerfeldt is desperate to see you, Rose. Please don't make your time in here longer than it has to be."

I turn and spit on him. "*You* put me in here!" I start yelling as he tries to speak. "I don't care, I don't care. You want me to behave? Am I not reacting to your liking? Should I stop yelling? Should I be a good little possession and sit and look pretty?" More spit is flying from my mouth by the end.

Joe leaves the room, but I continue to holler.

Part of me worries he'll get the feeding tube again. Or more of that poison to silence me. Still, I shout. "I want *out!* Do not talk to me about him! Don't you dare!"

I look toward the window—too high for me to reach, too small for me to climb through, even if I could somehow get the bars off it.

I muse over the idea of somehow fitting through it and falling to my death.

The door opens again and shuts, and I yell, "Get out!"

But the door doesn't open again, and I whip around, ready for more yelling.

When I see it's Abel, I want to rush to him, but I fall instead, unsteady, unable to lift myself properly in the straitjacket.

And he catches me before I hit the floor.

18 ABEL

"ABEL?"

I push her hair from her face and nod. I touch her cheeks and her face and even her lips because damn it, I can't fucking stop. "How are you feeling? I've been so fucking worried, Rose."

I want to kiss her. This is when I would kiss her, but I don't. I just press her into me, as if I can take her in my body. My ribs, my heart, my organs, they'd protect her. They'd keep her safe from these fucking people.

I hate the look in her eyes. I fucking hate that she's afraid and I can't do a thing for her. I can't protect her. I can't fight them off.

Rose is strong, but this place is killing her and all I want to do is save her.

I can't imagine a world without her now.

The worst part is, they might know this, and they might use it against us.

If that asshole letting me in here is any indication, they've caught on.

"Rose, baby, you have to do what they tell you to do, okay?"

She starts to shake her head, but I nod mine and squeeze her tighter. Her beautiful fucking face is inches from mine, so close I can feel the mugginess of her sweat and tears. She starts to wriggle but I'm not having that shit. She can't move much, and she can't touch me in this goddamn contraption.

Still, I grab her face as gently as I can. "Listen to me, if you want to get out of here, you have to. Besides, you can't leave me upstairs alone with all of those crazy fuckers." My smile is more of a question as I feel my eyes filling. *What is my fucking life now? What can I even do when she's suffering?*

She fucking *shines*, even in her misery.

I'll kill them all before I let them hurt her again.

"You do this," I whisper, pressing my lips to her cheek, "and I'll get us out of here. I promise, Rose. I *promise*, I'll get us out of here."

Her gasp turns into fresh tears and she nods. Her nod becomes this fervent action like it's sealing our deal. "I felt the walls closing in, but I couldn't count. This time, I didn't count." She sniffs.

And I run my fingers through her hair.

"I couldn't trick myself into thinking I was in control when I had no idea if you were okay," she says.

I'm not smart like Rose but I hear the things she isn't saying in the things she *is* saying. "I feel the same way," I whisper.

She sits in my arms until Dr. Brown walks in, minutes later. She's still warm with her waning rage but I only hope she'll trust me enough to listen to what they say. I can't break into solitary. They've got this fucking place secured by passcodes that I could never figure out. These aren't the kind of locks that a kid from around the way can pick.

But I figure, somewhere, someone isn't as careful as they should be. I'll find their mistake and I'll get us out of here.

I just hope she can keep it together until then.

Rose is released the next day. As soon as I see her, I want to hug her and kiss her and just fucking *run*.

She told me that I don't belong here. But *we* don't belong here because I belong wherever she is.

I wait for her to pick a table to sit at, but I hover close and ignore the staff who stare at us. To them, we're nothing.

It took seeing Rose in her violent glory to understand that this place doesn't care if we ever make it out.

We sit and she turns to me, her hands in her lap like she's a proper fucking princess and it makes me smile.

"When are we leaving?" she whispers, glancing around.

"It might take a little bit, but you have to try not to react to people. I don't know if they'll let you go next time."

She scoffs and rolls her eyes. The eyes that are already filling with tears. She's still an emotional mess and I don't want any of these assholes to see her this way.

A tserissen gemit iz shver tsum hailen, Ma would say.

A broken spirit is hard to heal.

"Go to the bathroom," I whisper. "I'll follow you there in a minute."

She nods and takes a moment to wipe her eyes before getting up.

That's it. Wipe your tears and tell them all to go to hell.

The nurses don't bother looking at me when she's not around. They blame it all on her, like I wasn't the one that put my hands on a staff member because I fucking wanted to. I want to tell them I'm my own fucking man and they'd do well to keep the fuck away from her. Bet that'd chap their fucking asses.

I get up and follow, hoping she isn't counting. I don't want her to ever feel that way again, like she can't find her comfort without me but maybe that's how it has to be for now.

Moments apart feel like someone has a goddamn bag over my head. I push the door open and there she stands, quiet and uncertain, her hands clutched in front of her.

I grab at one of them and when she winces, I look down. They're a fucking wreck, the nails jagged and bloody.

"What..." I look in her eyes, waiting for her to tell me what happened.

"I did this to myself," she says before choking on a sob. "Sometimes I feel so present and so much like...how steady you are. And then I'm a whole other monster and I don't know how I can take my next breath if I don't hurt someone."

I pull her into the handicap stall and shut the door. When I turn to face her, she's pressed against the wall, her eyes wide. It's like she knows I want to kiss her more than anything in my whole life. More than I even want to get the hell out of here.

"If I'm not allowed to be afraid of you, you don't get to be afraid of me," I tell her as I take one of her hands and turn it over. Her palms are smooth and unharmed, so I kiss the skin there before moving to each of her fingers. "I would never hurt you. And I don't think you'd hurt me."

Her eyes follow as I kiss her other fingers and she just stands there once I'm through. I sit on the floor with my back against the wall and she follows suit. We sit there silently for a few minutes. It's nice to just exist without eyes on us.

"What's the story behind your name?" she asks me.

Her question is completely unexpected, but I don't try to make sense of the way her mind works. "My ma named me Abel because she said my father was jealous of me and tried to kill me when she was pregnant. So, he was her Cain and I became her Abel." I don't tell her it's likely because he knew I wasn't his. It doesn't need to be said. "She was obsessed with the story for a long time. Said that was why she didn't have any other kids."

Rose is quiet, and she only looks ahead but I notice the way her chin quivers a little. "I'll kill him," she whispers, and I know she means it. Someone like Rose means it.

"He's long gone," I say. "Left after she died. But he wasn't around much to begin with."

We're quiet again and I'm listening to her breathing because even the sound of that makes me fucking happy.

"I have a list," she says.

I slide my palm against hers before interlocking our fingers.

"Doesn't everyone?" I ask, and she twists her lips and wiggles her nose a little. It makes it so hard not to kiss her.

"Not the way I do. I have so many people I'd kill if I were given the chance. And I'm not speaking hypothetically. I've thought about it, down to the weapon and the timing. My mother is at the top of the list."

Her mother?

"How would you do it?" My voice is low, and I don't want her to think I don't accept this part of her. I'd fucking accept all of her without judgment. I'd be her sanity, her clarity. It'd be my honor.

"Knife. Superficial wounds first. I'd slide my blade against her wrists horizontally. Listen to her scream because no one will hear her. Talk to her a little and tell her why this is happening."

I don't think she realizes that she's licked her lips a few times.

"And then, after listening to her beg and leading her to believe she has even a morsel of hope, I'd push my knife into her neck. Let the handle stick out and step back to admire my handiwork."

These are the things that make me wish Rose weren't in here. She has all day to plot these things. If I ever got us out of here, I wouldn't want her to waste time with her fucking list. Fuck that list.

She talks about it with a passion that I envy though. She can detail every moment of her fantasies with each person that's ever wronged her, and I can detail every moment of my fantasies with her.

I picture the way I'd touch her and kiss her. It'd be hard to keep from fucking mauling her, but I'd try. I'd kiss her pussy too, because girls like Rose deserve that.

I bet that if I sucked on her skin, it'd turn a pretty pink shade. *Like a rose.*

"Do I scare you?" she asks.

I stare at her because if she knew what I'd just been thinking, she'd probably be afraid of me. She doesn't scare me the way she scares other people. I'm not afraid of her viciousness. I'm afraid of whatever the fuck I'm feeling. "Not the way you think," I tell her because I don't know if she can handle the rest of what I'm thinking. "Do I scare you?"

She twists her lips again and this time, I do lean closer. Her eyes widen but she doesn't move away. Her body stays exactly where it is as I lean in to kiss her. My fingers press into her skin, where her jaw meets her neck and she licks her lips quickly.

Then it's just us. Lips against lips, skin against skin.

She offers up a peck at first, but I want more. Fuck, I want it all.

I press my lips against hers again and again and I don't back away. My lips move and my face tilts to have better access to her mouth. I feel her fingers slide under my shirt and dig into my back and drag toward my sides. I break the kiss to groan under the slight pain of her jagged nails against my bare skin before doubling back and kissing her with more force.

More, more, *more*.

I want to be more important than her list. I want her to fantasize about *me* the way I fantasize about her. I want to wrap her golden strands between my fingers and fuck the violence from her body.

But I also want to accept her the way she is.

I'm torn between wanting her to be normal and reminding myself that "normal" is a fucking nightmare. No one wants that shit. Fuck that.

I just want Rose. Her lips. Her body. Her love.

Her rage. Her thirst.

Take it out on my body, Rose. I'll be that for you.

She's still digging her nails into me and I'm still kissing her like I'm fucking her mouth with mine.

She's starting to pull back and I let her go. We're both out of breath but I lean back, and I look at her.

I like the way she looks, all flustered and dazed. I like the way she looks, knowing I made her look that way. Her lips are swollen because of me. Her eyes are wide because of me. She's flushed and pressing her thighs together because of me.

"I didn't think I was..." she whispers before launching herself at me again.

And while we kiss, I feel like I'm closer to the person I was before coming here. I can feel shit and my body is fucking *humming* with a need that I hadn't realized I had inside.

I feel like a whole person again. Less like a ghost and more like a solidified being.

Basherte, I think as I run my fingers through her hair and stare at her. *She has to be.*

But she's a Gentile, Ma would say. *A shikse. Her hair is too blonde, like the Nazis.*

She is golden and rosy, and I am her fucking puppet.

I would do anything for this ruthless girl.

19 ROSE

I can't stop kissing Abel. I'd never found so much appeal in the idea of pressing my mouth to another individual's for the sake of lust or some fleeting sentiment. Not until he touched his lips to mine like he was asking a question.

Or taking the answer from me.

I'm not as skilled as he is when it comes to letting my body express my emotions, but that doesn't bother me. He makes me feel too good to worry about anything other than what his tongue is doing with mine; a slow roll that is somehow mimicked deep in my abdomen. He makes me feel like he might be mine to keep, after all.

He quiets the constant roar in my head and makes it sound more like a lullaby; something that could maybe come second to him.

His fingers curl against my cheek and slide down to graze the side of my breast. If I ever lit someone on fire, it wouldn't hold a candle to how hot my skin feels right now.

"You're everything I imagined."

His lips move down to my neck as he says those words and I shiver against him, my hands in his hair. Those soft locks brush over my skin as he moves his tongue over my pulse. *How is this feeling so sensational?* He's rolling his taste buds over my skin like I'm some sort of delicacy.

We've been in here for what feels like hours and when someone enters the restroom, Abel presses his fingertips against my lips as he climbs on the toilet seat. I'm still sitting on the floor and I'm happily stunned, immobile, weakened by him.

"Ms. Montgomery?"

My eyes shoot to the stall door and I clear my throat. "I'm not feeling well," I lie.

"Do you need anything?"

Her voice is getting closer and I start to panic. "No. Just leave me alone!"

I look up at Abel and he shrugs, tilting his flattened hand to one side and then the other, his lips pressed firmly together as if he's telling me to be nicer. *Fine.*

"Please," I add. "I'll be out soon."

"Are you sure?"

I stand and open the stall door.

The nurse backs away quickly, knocking into the paper towel dispenser.

"I'll be out shortly."

She nods and turns away to walk out. Once I see she's gone, I lock myself back in the stall. Abel is already climbing down from the toilet and I yank him to me, cutting off his chuckle with a kiss.

Kiss.

One word, four letters, and I feel like it's not enough. The English language should've spared more letters. Maybe all twenty-six, used several times.

It shouldn't take something named with four letters to change my whole world but that's where I am now. Looking at things a little differently.

All because I've been kissed by a man who's promised to set me free.

I CAN'T SLEEP. Instead, I turn over and over in my bed, sure that hours have passed and nearly wishing I counted them because I wish Abel were here. I look over at the windows, one of its bars half covering the moon from my vantage point.

There's a sound at my door but when I look over, I see no one.

My door opens, and I frown because the nurse has already done her bed check.

When I see Abel, I jump off the bed and hug him. "What are you doing?" I whisper. "They could've caught you."

He shakes his head and pushes the door shut behind him. "I've already figured out which ways to go to avoid the cameras." He places his hands on my cheeks and presses a quick hard kiss to my mouth. "I promised you I'd get us outta here and I'm working on it. I'll get you out of here, Rose."

I kiss him softer and he steps forward so I have no choice but to step back. This happens, step after step, until I'm being lowered onto my bed. My hands reach for the skin beneath his shirt again and I feel the lines my nails made earlier. I reach higher on his back, so I'm running my fingers down his spine and he takes my lower lip between his teeth. A gentle tug unlike the way I drag my nails against his skin. I am rough and relentless, and he is romantic and *real*.

When he rolls his hips into mine, I gasp, and he pulls away with a grin.

"I'm not gonna fuck you, Rose. Not today, anyway." He pulls my arms away from his body, sets them on the bed with determination, and drops a kiss to my forehead. "Not today. But definitely someday."

He's out of my room quickly and quietly. Only the way his natural scent lingers proves that I hadn't dreamed of his presence.

Can words reach out and touch you?

Can they stroke you and make your skin heat with something you've never felt before?

Desire.

Are words capable of such things?

Every moment with Abel makes him seem more and more like some mythical creature that can love a monster.

No, Abel is a mythical creature that can make a monster fall in love with *him*.

20 ABEL

FOR THE PAST WEEK, I TIPTOED THROUGH THE QUIET halls of Silverwing while the other patients slept, trying to figure out how the hell we'd get out of here. Night after night, I watched the night shift nurses and janitors. The first night, one of the janitors left a stairwell door open, the same one Dr. Brown and I had snuck out of. I witnessed one of the male nurses taking one of the patients through there and into the hallway. They came back disheveled and I wanted to punch this fucker for dipping his dick into the crazy pool.

Even though I had every intention of doing it with Rose.

The second night, the janitor left the door unlocked again but this time, he joined the male nurse in the hallway with one of the patients. The janitor does this every night and nearly every night, the male nurse takes one of the girls to the stairwell.

I think about Rose and if this has ever happened to her. Her room is on the opposite end of the wing. The only thing separating Rose from these perverts is their laziness.

I remind myself again that I want to fuck Rose. But that's different. She's coherent and I want to fuck her with her *permission*. Like a fucking sane person.

Every night, I watch them around the same time, praying the nurses don't change their bed check timing. I jump back into my bed in time for a nurse to stick their face in the room and then leave. They typically only check once during the night, which is so fucking stupid. Then I watch the janitor again, trying to figure out what kind of time frame we'll be working with. If we leave after the bed checks, we'll have a lot more time to get out of the area if the male nurse doesn't decide to get his rocks off early.

Before I head back to bed for the night, I check on Rose, picking the locks with ease since I'd found hair pins near the nurses' station one night.

Rose is usually waiting up for me most nights but when she's asleep, I just kiss her forehead and go back to my room.

Every morning feels like hell after staying up nearly all night. I try not to fall asleep and Rose helps with her presence and her questions.

"You've never asked me why I want to kill my mother." Even her statement sounds like a fucking question.

I smile. "If you wanted me to know, you would've told me," I say with a shrug.

Rose's eyes sparkle with the same excitement she had the first day I got here. It makes me want to go back and relive it all over again. And who the fuck wants to do that? A lovesick *putz*, that's who.

"She's the reason I'm here," she says.

I look just past her and when I see that the nurses aren't looking at us, I feel like I accomplished something. It took months for them to get the fuck over us. I focus on Rose again and she continues.

"I think both inadvertently and then later, with rather cruel intentions. My parents fought all the time and sometimes my mother would have a black eye, or my father would have a gash on his cheek. Still, somehow the world thought they were perfect."

Her green eyes are so far away that I want to remind her that

I'm here and I'm not going anywhere. They'd have to pry my dead fucking body from her.

"My mother's life was so chaotic, and she only wanted to leave. I think that's why she didn't pay me or Grace much mind. Other than when she wanted us to play the perfect daughters, anyway. She didn't pay any mind when I'd hit the kids at school. She was always paying off the dean and that worked, until I got to high school. The last girl was unrecognizable when I was through with her and I got expelled. Nearly got arrested but my father stepped in that time. That was when I started therapy and they gave my rage a name. I got a tutor and took up home schooling, but they should've known it was only a matter of time."

I'm listening so closely that I almost miss the way her eyes start to look glassy.

"My parents were fighting again, and my mother came down, screaming that she wanted to leave him. He told her if she left, she couldn't have any money. They didn't talk about their children, just the money." She shakes her head. "That should've been my first clue, but my mother came into my room that night and asked me..."

Under the table, I grab her hand.

"She asked me to kill my father."

Don't react, don't react, don't you fucking *react.* I keep my face impassive as she continues.

"She told me no one would know, and we'd split the insurance money. She told me he wasn't a good man, that he cheated on her and beat her and made her have sex with him when she didn't want to."

What kind of asshole mother tells this to her child? I squeeze her hand.

"So, I went into their room with a silver candlestick—I'm almost certain it was a wedding gift—and hit him over the head with it, several times. Until I was too tired to continue. And, of course, my mother lied. She denied ever telling me to kill him and everything she'd ever covered up came to light."

She squeezes my hand back. Her bottom lip is caught between her teeth for a moment before she starts talking again.

"She fed me lies and unleashed my anger on my father. And now she lives with his fortune, free. I always tell Joe that I don't feel regret or remorse but I don't know how true that is. My father wasn't innocent, but his end wasn't something that should've come from me."

"Do you think your ma lied to you?"

"Not about all of it. But she failed to admit her faults and now my sister's stuck with her. If there's any good I can do for Grace, it'd be getting rid of the evil woman I left her with. So, she has to die."

"You sure you won't regret it?"

She smiles but it's like that fucking monster in her is doing it. "Oh, no. This is something I've *dreamed* about doing."

I want to ask her who else is on her list, but I don't.

I'm sure I'll find out soon enough.

I WANT TO LEAVE TONIGHT. I don't tell Rose, but I have everything planned. I stare at her as she pushes her oatmeal around her bowl, wondering if she knows this is the last time she'll be eating that shit for breakfast. She looks up and catches me staring. She doesn't smile coyly the way the other girls do. She doesn't even smile. She just stares back at me like we're having a conversation no one else can hear.

"When I first saw you, I thought you looked like a villain," she says.

It's like she fucking *knows* this is it. No more Silverwing and no more shitty fucking oatmeal and no more of these damn rules where I can't touch her even when it's killing me not to.

"When I first saw you, I thought you looked like a goddess." I remember it so clearly. All gold and lonely and beautiful.

"And now what do you think?" she asks.

"Now? Now I just think you're...my *sheyn royz*."

It's then that she smiles, in a way that looks like a secret. "That means rose in..."

"Yiddish," I finish for her. "And it means 'beautiful rose'."

"If you think I'm beautiful now, you should've seen me before. Primped to perfection, just the way my mother liked."

"A little makeup doesn't change the way you look completely." *Right?*

She laughs. "I don't think so. But it makes me look a little *more*, I guess."

"More?"

"Longer lashes, pinker lips..."

"Pinker than they already are?" My eyes are on her mouth that already looks so goddamn perfect, untouched. If anything, they look better after I've spent an hour kissing them. Stick *that* in your fucking makeup bag.

I think about Rose before she came here, and I wonder what she did in her free time. "What's your favorite thing to do? Besides think of ways to kill people," I say with a grin. Fucked up pair that we are.

"Well, before I came here, I thought I'd do something with numbers. I've always been really good with numbers," she says.

"No, that's shit. I'm talking about things that make you feel alive."

"Besides talking to you?"

Well, melt my fucking heart.

"I like—liked—to sew," she says. "Make my own clothes, blankets, bags. All kinds of things, really. And when I wore the things I made, I always felt proud. Until my mother made me stop. She said if it wasn't name brand, it didn't belong on my body."

"Your ma sounds like a real fucking piece of work, you know."

"If anyone knows, it's me," she says as she pushes her forgotten oatmeal away. She licks her hand where some spilled, and my eyes are on her mouth.

Of course.

I've thought about fucking her more times than I'd care to admit. I've thought about the way she feels when I kiss her and then I multiply that by a thousand.

I wonder what the sex would be like. Maybe I'd never find out, but I've jacked off at night to the idea of it. Those perfect pink lips around my dick. Her ass up as I fuck her from behind. Her fingernails leaving even more marks on my skin so when I shower, they sting, and I remember how they got there. And it gets me hard all over again because she feels just that fucking good.

My poor socks never had a goddamn chance.

I imagine all of that golden hair between my fingers.

In my mind, she likes pain. She dishes it out because she can fucking take it.

Maybe I'd never know but my imagination grows as wild as she is.

She's staring at me and I'm just happy she can't see my stiff dick in these loose pants.

She gets up to take her food to the trash and my eyes fly to her ass.

Of course.

When she comes back, she tucks her hair behind her ears and starts in on a brand new string of questions. "Do you have the same last name as your father?"

I shake my head. "I never wondered about it until I got old enough to know other kids' families all had the same last name. I didn't know the reason Kevin Baker didn't give me his last name was because he thought my ma was a whore."

She doesn't react, just soaks the facts in.

This girl, born with a silver spoon in her mouth, can listen to a sorry son of a bitch's story and not pass judgment.

I never thought I'd see the day where I could be this fucking *open* with another human being, let alone a girl I'm insanely attracted to. But it's more than attraction.

Basherte, my ma would insist.

All while Rose continues with her questions, the word rings in my head.

Basherte, basherte, basherte.

21 ROSE

I WANT TO STAY AWAKE, SO I CAN SEE ABEL AFTER HE does his nightly reconnaissance, but my eyes are closing, no matter how hard I try to fight it.

I feel as though I've only slept for a minute when someone is shaking me awake and I sit up. It's dark and quiet, the room full of shadows, but Abel's voice slices through the darkness before I can react.

"Rose, baby, it's time to go."

He calls me "baby" and I don't want to be called anything other than that by him. I don't register what else he said for a moment because I'm held captive by that one word—*baby*.

He tugs me from the bed because I haven't gotten up on my own. I glance around the room, but I don't have anything I want to bring with me. This place has taken enough from me and I'm ready to leave it all behind. I clench my fists and they ache from my time in solitary, but they also remind me that all I have in my future—if I remain here—is pain.

I think about Joe as we tiptoe through the halls, following some sort of jagged path to avoid the cameras.

I wonder if he'll miss me, if our years together meant anything to him. I am quick to dismiss emotions. At least I was, until I got a taste of my own all because of the guy I'm running behind.

We turn a corner and Abel slows down in front of me. I glance at him, with the question in my eyes. *Is this it?*

He gestures around another corner, to the right, and I peer down the hallway.

The door is ever so slightly ajar at the end of the hall.

"It can't be this easy," I whisper to him.

He only shakes his head for a moment before I see someone coming from the other end of the hall.

Two people.

As they near, I see it's Allison and one of the night nurses.

She's shaking her head as he pulls her closer to the door. When she starts to pull away, he yanks her to him and covers her mouth with his hand. I hear a whisper of a sob and my hands start to shake.

Allison doesn't deserve what he's about to do to her.

"We have to do something," I tell Abel as another man enters the door and closes it behind him.

"We can't risk it," he whispers back to me.

But I don't care. I step out from our hiding place and charge down the hall. The closer I get, the more shuffles and grunts I hear.

Then arms are bound around my waist. I try to jerk away, but Abel refuses to relent.

"You need to calm the fuck down," he says, his words hot against my ear.

This odd sensation pulsates through me, from my chest, down to where my hips don't meet my legs. Only space, wanting too badly to be filled by Abel.

I hear a thud against the door and I try one last time, in vain, to get away. "Do *something*," I practically beg him. *Anything* to keep the monster from coming out and ruining our plans.

"Fine." He sets me down and looks around.

I've gotten to know Abel in our time here. I know his poor

language skills and his terrible upbringing. But I also know that he is often underestimated, looked at as some idiot. But Abel is the smartest kind of man: resourceful and quick on his feet. *He'll get us out of here.*

"Stay here," Abel tells me.

But before he slinks away, I grab his arm. "What are you doing?"

"Providing a distraction."

He's gone before I can ask him what he's going to do. I watch him disappear around the corner and look back at the door.

Without him here, it's so much easier...

I rush toward the door and yank it open. Allison is against the wall, the male nurse thrusting into her. I grab him by the back of his neck and push him with as much force as I can down the stairs.

Once he hits the bottom, he's still, his mouth ajar and his eyes glassy and vacant; his head is angled unnaturally away from his neck.

Allison is quiet as she turns to look into my eyes, her chest heaving. I want to brush her hair from her sweaty face and welcome her. My monster would love the company.

But I refrain as I watch her adjust her pants so they cover her once more.

The exit sign paints us all red and I think to myself, *my righteous red. My righteous vengeance.*

I hear someone coming down the stairs. The second man who'd entered the stairwell—a janitor by the looks of it—takes one look at the two of us and turns to leave.

I'm surprised to see Allison grab him first. She throws all of her weight on him and when he falls, she kicks and kicks him. I want to tell her to stop screaming like a madwoman, but that's what sweet violence does: it shows us who we are.

She is so beautifully painted in her truth—hair wild, mouth open in triumph.

Blood, dark and slow moving, leaks from his body and I step

away, pushing away from the wall I hadn't realized I was leaning on.

Once I'm back outside the door, with no sign of Abel, I start to count.

One, two, three...

The hall is still empty, and I edge back toward the corner we'd started at.

Fifteen, sixteen...

I hear someone carrying keys. They're coming down the hall and if they see me, that's the end of this. I'll never make it out of here. My hands ache at the thought.

Not after the events in the stairwell. Not ever.

Twenty-nine, thirty, thirty-one...

I try to breathe quietly but with each footfall, I'm closer to more time in solitary. More counting. More Joe and more nurses pricking me and leaving marks on my body.

I'll kill this person in order to avoid that fate.

Thirty-six, thirty-seven...

The keys jingle closer and I'm bracing myself when I hear a shriek. The person headed my way stops, turns, and runs the way they came.

The fire alarm sounds and I only hope Abel hasn't been caught. I'm about to walk back into the stairwell when I feel a hand reach out and grab me, pulling me away from the wall.

"Let's go," Abel says, his voice breathless.

I can barely hear him over the shrieking of the alarm. He pushes me, and we start running. As we enter the stairwell, I try not to stop and rejoice.

"The fuck happened here?" he asks but doesn't stop.

Not even as we see a sobbing Allison still kicking the janitor's dead body. And not when we step over the other dead body at the bottom of the landing.

Our steps are light, Abel is pressing his index finger against his lips, but we're moving as fast as possible. We hit the final landing and Abel is illuminated by the fluorescent lights and the red exit sign above the door he's about to push open.

I want to remember him this way forever—eyes hopeful, grin boyish, touch guiding.

But he pushes the door open and the moment is gone. And so is the sound of the fire alarm.

I'm breathing in fresh air and I want to celebrate but Abel takes my hand and we keep running.

Running away from the cattle farm and into the world where I can be whomever I'd like.

I'm not thinking about anything other than how amazing this moment feels.

22 ABEL

ROSE IS STARING AT ME, HER EYES WIDE AND HER mouth open, lips tilted up just a little.

It isn't just any kind of staring or the creepy kind that makes you feel uncomfortable. It's the kind that makes you want to get up and conquer the motherfucking world. Like her happiness is based on mine or something.

I glance over at her a few times, trying to see if she looks any different now that we're free, but also trying to keep from busting my ass in front of her.

She turns her gaze away from me as we continue running, a little slower the farther we get from Silverwing. Her face is tipped to the sky as we finally make it to the clearing.

She soaks up the moon like it feeds her and I have no idea what we're doing next.

Rose doesn't look worried. At all.

We slow to a walk and I'm looking around, trying to come up with a plan.

I have no fucking clue.

I honestly wasn't sure I'd even be able to get us this far.

It was entirely too easy.

I look back, expecting to see a sign that someone is following us.

No lights bouncing around, the way men running with flash-lights would look, no sounds of footsteps or yelling.

Only dark, silent trees look back at me.

"Why are you frowning?"

Her face is free of concern, not an ounce of fear on her.

She's fucking beautiful.

"Trying to figure out what to do next, *basherte*."

We're still making our way through the clearing when I hear an engine rumbling up ahead. It's been so long since I heard an engine and this one sounds like it's another mile away from falling to shit.

I run a little faster and step out onto the road, just as a pick-up truck revs past, so close, the ends of my hair dance dangerously. "Holy fuck," I say, just as I'm jerked back by the collar of my shirt.

The truck comes to a stop a few yards away.

Rose lets go of my shirt and up ahead, the truck driver's door squeaks open. I can't see the person until they're almost halfway past their truck, heading our way.

"What the hell is wrong with you?" a voice almost as hard on my ears as the engine rings out. The man walking toward us is all gut, his long hair tied back, and his eyes full of anger. "What kinda psychos are you, coming outta the goddamn woods like that? I coulda killed you or gone off the goddamn road!"

Rose moves to step forward, but I hold my arm out, keeping her in place.

I don't need to look at her to know she's ready for whatever bullshit comes our way. I can feel how tense she is; her presence alone feels like a fucking threat.

"We need help," I tell the man. He's closer and I can see the silver strands highlighting his dark hair and the crow's feet at the ends of his eyes that would be showing, if he were smiling. But we aren't that lucky.

He's a mean looking son of a bitch.

Ma would complain. Say he's being an *alter cocker* as she takes a swig of beer and spits a little at him.

"That's obvious. The pair of ya standing out here, no shoes on, looking crazy as all hell." His voice sounds more like a growl than anything.

I drop my arm, hoping maybe if he doesn't see either of us as a threat, he'll get us far away from Silverwing.

He pauses for a moment and I have no idea what to make of this fucked up situation. We *are* standing here looking crazy as hell. But the only thing in my mind, ringing louder and louder, is that we need to get the fuck out of here. "We need a way out of here."

The man twists his lips as he stares at Rose, ignoring me.

I wonder what he sees when he looks at her.

I know I look like an asshole. But Rose, she looks like she was made by the sun. All light and intensity.

But he doesn't know she could burn just as fucking hot.

I look at her, from her expressionless face, to her fists at her sides, down her legs.

Blood.

On her pants, and on her feet.

Fuuuuckkkkk.

"You'd best get going. After I call the cops, there won't be much time for you to get very far." He turns to get back in his truck.

He's almost to the cab door when Rose shoots past me.

She's slamming the door on his body for the second time before I get my head out of my ass and reach her. His body slumps and he slides out a little, his head in the door jam. I'm wrestling her away but she shoves me and kicks the door so it bounces off his skull.

"Rose!" I've all but mimicked the goddamn wrestlers on TV with the ways I'm attempting to restrain her, scared as shit that she'll turn on me. "What the fuck?" I grunt when I get an elbow to my stomach and double over. My arms band around my center in a shitty attempt to ease the pain.

"Abel?" Her voice sounds uncertain.

And I hold one of my hands out to keep her from touching me. "I'm fine," I tell her, my voice a little raspier than usual.

Shit. This is already starting off badly.

"We have to go." I stand straight and attempt to shake it off.

Rose stares at me, disheveled and perfect. "Did I hurt you?" she whispers. Her eyes are wide, her hands are clutched in front of her.

If it were anyone else, any other fucking person, I'd give them my anger, my sarcasm. I wouldn't spare even an ounce.

But with Rose, I only assure her that I'm fine again before I check the man's pulse. It's faint, but it's there.

I'd prefer if we didn't start our new lives with murder.

I reach into his pockets and draw out his wallet.

But I'll start with theft.

Rose and I drag his body off the road, toward the woods, hidden amongst the trees.

It's strange to think he and I are about to trade places.

That this life I am choosing with Rose will not be without cost.

People will get hurt if they get in our way.

People will probably even die.

And they'll definitely suffer, I think to myself as we get in the truck. Rose barely has her seatbelt on before I'm damn near pressing the gas through the floor.

The trees are flying past, the truck shaking, the engine so loud we won't be able to talk unless we yell over it.

We're fucking reeling.

We're fucking *free*.

After a half hour of driving, I pull into a closed gas station and take stock.

His wallet holds eighty-four dollars and a picture of a smiling little girl.

It does something inside me, twists my heart a little.

He'll probably die on the side of the road, and that little girl will have a hole in her world.

That hole will be *our* fault.

"What does *basherte* mean?" Rose whispers the question.

And I blink because what the fuck? But then I remember I called her that while we were running. "It's Yiddish. Like a soul mate, I guess. Or fate. That's how my ma explained it anyway."

Rose kinda squints and I shrug.

"The idea of having a soul mate is ridiculous." She peers over at me. "But I suppose if I had a soul mate, it'd be you, Abel."

Just like that, my heart untwists itself.

I'm not entirely sure what's next, but it'd be a hell of a lot worse without her.

And I'm reminded why we're even here to begin with.

My hands reach for her before my brain registers what I'm doing. I don't care that she's covered in blood from more than one person, I don't care that we're both tired and have no fucking clue what comes next. I don't care.

Not as I press my lips to hers. The first is a soft question.

The next is a certain answer.

She sighs into my mouth and digs her nails into my skin.

"We did it," I say between kisses.

She nods once, a little one that doesn't force us apart.

When I sit back, I glance around, trying to figure out which way we should go. We've been sitting here long enough.

I push the key back into the ignition.

Before I turn it, I glance over at her.

Her eyes are on the full moon outside, her body leaning toward the windshield. "We're free," she whispers.

"Yeah. And we have to keep moving, if we want to stay that way," I tell her.

"We need to find my mother," she says, her eyes still on the moon in wonder. "Head toward Utica."

My lips press together, to keep the words I want to say from forcing their way out.

You don't need to do this shit, Rose. You have me.

When I turn the truck on and pull off, I take a right out of the gas station parking lot.

Not two miles down the road, a sign tells us that Utica is thirty-five miles from here.

Rose grabs my hand and squeezes.

I'm a fucking idiot for feeling jealous, for wishing she was this excited about *us*, but I squeeze her hand back as we rumble down the road toward Rose's revenge.

WE'D DRIVEN another hour when I take an exit into a small town. The sun is coming up and it looks like one of those stupid ass Norman Rockwell paintings like my ma used to have on a plate before I told her it was a Christmas painting.

She threw it out the window, her drunk ass never having realized it for herself.

I see a shopping center on the right and pull inside the parking lot, hoping one of the stores is open.

When I look over at Rose, after parking the truck, I realize she's asleep. *Good.* The last thing I need is her coming inside with me, blood on her pants and now her shirt.

A big ass sigh escapes my lips and I scrub my hands over my face. Facial hair has never really been an issue for me, it grows only enough to look like I'd been dabbling in someone's pubes, but in my time at Silverwing, a few more whiskers had appeared on my chin. I feel them now as I try to gain a sense of *I didn't just fuck my whole life up.*

She's still sleeping when I hop out of the truck.

My clothes feel gross, sticking to me and doing not a fucking thing to keep the cold breeze from slapping the shit out of me. I hadn't noticed the cold before.

Adrenaline, dumbass.

We have to figure our shit out quickly. It's too cold to be wandering around without warmer clothes or some sort of shelter.

I have the cash tucked into my waistband and as I enter the store I wonder if I'll bother spending it or just exercise my five-finger discount.

It's even fucking colder in here than it is outside. I shiver, ignoring the way my now dingy socks feel, damp and loose.

Ma would pop me upside the head for walking around looking like this.

That blonde devil has you walking around, dressed in shamatta, *like some kind of homeless person.*

"I was homeless, Ma," I mutter under my breath.

The woman standing at the register shoots me a strange look and it feels like déjà vu. The way people looked at me at the crazy house before I even got to Silverwing, when they had to decide if I was going to off myself or not.

And then they sent me to rot at Silverwing, all because they wanted me to remember standing on that balcony.

I don't fess up to shit I don't do.

The woman is still watching as I take a deep breath and walk toward the clothing section.

I've had to be a decent thief in order to survive. But the woman at the register finds her way toward me, just as I realize I have no fucking clue what size Rose wears. Not in clothes, not in panties, not in shoes.

So I grab whatever the fuck I can for us, enough so that we aren't riding around looking like two escapees—which is exactly what the fuck I feel like as this woman damn near breathes down my neck—and I head to the register.

It takes half our money, but nothing beats the feeling of peeling off these dirty ass socks on my way out and tossing them on the ground just as I slip my feet into slippers.

I hear the woman yell after me, but she can kiss my fucking ass for all the dirty looks she gave me while she rang me up.

When I look up at the truck, I see Rose standing just in front of it.

"Get in the truck, Rose," I tell her, my patience running thin on low sleep and stress over what the fuck would happen next.

"I thought you left me," she says, her voice quiet. But it doesn't crack, doesn't waver. She is confidently vulnerable and it's the strangest fucking thing.

I sigh as I head to her side of the truck. I toss the bag on the hood and pull her close. "Now why would I do that, *sheyn royz?*"

Her pretty pink lips poke out just a little, and I'm fucking weak for her. I couldn't leave her. Not now, not even if she tried to push me out the goddamn door.

"We have to go," I whisper before pressing a kiss to her lips and then another. "You need to not look as fucking insane as you do right now."

We get in the truck and I pull off, just in time for the woman inside to step out, a phone pressed to her ear.

23 ROSE

FREEDOM.

The last time I was free, I was wearing pajamas that cost more money than the amount we'd taken from the old man's wallet.

But I wasn't this happy.

I've never been as content as I am now.

"Where are we going?" I yell over the sound of the engine.

Abel looks over at me, a small smile gracing his face. As handsome as he is, he still has that devilish expression about him, whether his face is displaying pleasure or no emotion at all.

Abel, the one who would try to ask someone for help before simply taking what he needs, looks the way I should. Like some sort of threat.

"We need to shower and change," he yells back, punctuating the last word with a long yawn. "And get some sleep."

He says the last bit low, but I read his lips.

I felt guilty as soon as I'd woken up. And then a bit panicky when I'd noticed I was alone in the parked truck, with no sign of Abel in sight.

When I saw him come out of the store with a bag in his hand

and slippers on his feet, I wanted to rush to him, the way I feel most women would do to the men in their lives.

But most women are filled with romantic love when committing that gesture.

Meanwhile, for me, it would've been an act of relief, my anxiety having dissipated at the sight of him.

Would I ever be able to perform romantic acts for Abel?

My eyes land on the hands that grip the steering wheel. There are a few scars on them, small like the ones adorning my arms from my time in Silverwing.

Abel saved me from collecting more.

Abel saved me from looking in the mirror and wondering where the time went, how I got to grow so much in such a small cage.

He saved me from having to kill for the last time in an attempt to never become one of those animals who die in captivity.

Never again.

Filled to the brim with gratitude, I reach for his hand, figuring I could start there.

A few minutes later, we're pulling into a parking lot. I stare at the building in front of us once he parks.

"A gym?" I ask.

He shrugs. "I saw the sign on the highway. We need to shower."

My lips are pressed together as he faces me. I'm still staring at the building when he touches my chin and turns my head so I'm facing him. "We need money," I whisper.

"We need to get out of here," he whispers back as he starts to twirl strands of my hair.

I feel his breath on my face, he's so close. He said this earlier, and his worry concerns me. Still…

"I know where we can find money," I say.

"Where?"

I look him in the eye. "My mother."

Abel opens his mouth and shuts it. It's moments like these that

I don't quite know what to think. I fall between knowing what he's thinking and not knowing a thing at all.

"Are you thinking about it?" he asks.

I don't want to lie to him. He deserves the truth. *But can he handle it?* He's saddled with me now. There are no walls to keep me from doing what I told him I wanted to do. "Yes."

He runs the backs of his fingers against my cheek. "Is it not enough to be free?"

I close my eyes. This is what he wants, what I don't know I can ever give him. "I don't know that it ever will be."

It feels like his eyes are trying to dig the truth from me so that's what I give him. This is me. I am no one's angel. I will crave blood no matter how many sweet kisses he gives me. I will never change.

"Our dog bit me once and I beat him so hard, I broke his bones. I think that's when it started for me. My mother buried him and never said a word." I tell him these things without emotion, hardly remembering whether I reacted afterwards or not. All I remember is the way my emotions felt like fire. Then after, like I'd been dipped in cool water.

I remember the rage, the flash of red, and then the need to retaliate. He ended up having to get put to sleep. After that, we couldn't have any more pets. My mother claimed it was too heart-breaking when they died but I knew it was because she sensed something in me.

Her daughters were beautiful. Her daughters were perfect.

But one of them was evil.

Abel is silent for a moment. Then he's pressing another sweet kiss to my lips and getting out of the truck.

I follow, like I hope he always will.

24 ABEL

WE SNEAK PAST THE FRONT DESK AND HEAD TOWARD the locker rooms.

"I know there's one for boys and one for girls, but we'll stick together," I tell Rose as I lead her into the men's room. It's empty, of course and I tell her to shower first as I take a bench and push it under the door's handle.

When I turn, I see a flash of naked skin.

Fucking hell.

I squeeze my eyes shut and turn away. When I open them again, I still see her.

I look away, not realizing the mirrors across the room would give me the perfect view of her naked back. I damn near stand taller, on the tips of my fucking toes, just to get a glimpse of her ass. She enters the shower and closes the curtain before I can get a good look.

I expect her to take long, but she doesn't. She doesn't hum, she doesn't take her time feeling the luxury of a shower that isn't timed, doesn't rejoice in her privacy.

Group showers at Silverwing had been a fucking nightmare.

This was not how I'd expect our first showers to be. Then again,

I never expected we'd be in a gym locker room, either.

She slides the shower curtain open and I don't look in the mirror or back at her.

"Abel?"

My eyes are squeezed shut again. "Yeah?"

She's silent, then says, "I need something to dry my hair."

I glance up and she's pulled a shirt over her wet skin and I can see her tits.

Holy shit, I can see her perfect fucking tits and she probably has no idea.

Fuck. Me.

"Abel?" Her voice is so sweet sounding that it somehow manages to lift my eyes to hers.

"Huh?"

"I need something," she says, gesturing toward her dripping wet hair.

Immediately, I pull off my shirt and hand it to her. Wordlessly, I take the rest of my clothes off and slip past her. Her fucking eyes are burning holes into my body but I'm just glad to return the favor. I'm sporting a semi after seeing her hard nipples damn near puncture her t-shirt.

Shit.

I will not rub one out while she's just outside the shower.

We don't have time for this shit.

Shit.

I grab the generic soap and lather it all over my body before letting the near scalding water wash the suds away. I keep my head under the water for a little, hoping it'll wake up my senses and somehow put my dick to sleep.

When I turn off the water, the bathroom is still quiet. I open the shower curtain and see Rose standing a few feet away in front of the sinks with the mirrors above them. The same mirror that I tried to check her ass out in. She's watching me, her eyes flicking to my face and down my naked body before sliding right back up to my eyes, as she brushes her teeth.

I shake my head a little, reaching for the clean clothes and tugging them over my damp skin, which is a pain in the fucking ass. As I fight with my clothes, she's pulling on a large plaid shirt that makes her look like a lumberjack.

I slide my feet into the slippers that don't fit me but I don't care. Better than being fucking barefoot. I don't even have socks on, which probably isn't a good idea unless I want to catch some sort of fungus, but I've lived this life already. I know what to expect. I look up at Rose—who's braided her hair—and hope she's willing to chase the lows and highs with me.

She holds out the toothbrush she was just using as she spits. I grab it from her and she explains, "You only bought one."

I run my finger over the wet bristles with a grin. "There are worse things I could put in my mouth, Rose."

My hair is still dripping and as I press toothpaste from one of the travel sized tubes on the counter, I feel her step behind me. I shove the toothbrush in my mouth and look at her as she starts drying the ends of my hair with my old shirt.

I try to smile around the toothbrush but she's too focused to see anything other than the task at hand.

I finish brushing my teeth and she steps back—content with her work—as I finish up.

"Thanks," I say after spitting the froth from my mouth. I see a lone wire hanger against the window and I grab it quickly, bending it and tucking it in the back of my jeans. She only smiles as she watches me, not knowing we'll likely have to steal a car in the near future.

"You're welcome."

It's hard to believe this girl could harm anyone, let alone kill them. And maybe that's what makes her so fucking dangerous.

She's a Venus flytrap, hidden in a rose's body, I think to myself as I take her hand in mine.

. . .

"SO, WHAT'S THE PLAN?" Rose asks, her voice without worry. It's strange to hear her so carefree as she walks in cheap flip flops.

I glance down at them and back at her smiling face. "You said your ma had money. Think we can make it there before people start waking up?"

Rose shakes her head. "But it doesn't matter. She won't be home." Her eyes get all glassy and faraway looking. "Maybe Grace will be home."

"Grace?"

Rose nods, her eyes still somewhere else. "My little sister. I told you about her, remember?" Her hand reaches out and presses lightly into my chest. "Can she come with us?"

"Uh…" *Two of them?* I can barely handle Rose as it is. *Christ.*

"My mother kept her from me." She blinks. "I'd like to save her."

The good boy in me says that murder is wrong. But the man in me that's fallen for Rose makes me want to kill her mother myself. For the look on Rose's face. But I know myself. I know I wouldn't. But thinking about it makes me feel a fuck ton happier. "We have to try to make it before anyone notices we've left. They'll call her and then we'll be fucked. We have to take advantage of the fact that no one knows we're gone."

Shit, they probably already know and have alerted the authorities. We're probably too late anyway.

"In less than twelve hours, we've escaped a mental institute, assaulted a man, stole his truck and wallet, and snuck into a gym locker room," I say. "Should we add breaking and entering to the list?"

"I'm okay with that."

I grin. "Of course you are," I say and press a kiss to her mouth.

We don't have a thing in our possession other than the clothes on our backs but somehow, we have to make it out of here. We're

running out of time. I don't want to pull her into any more criminal activity but I can't come up with any other fucking way.

We gather our things and head outside toward the truck.

Her smile should worry me. I should be worried about what the
hell freedom is gonna do to her but in this moment, I don't give a
shit. I've never felt like this. Like she'll be by my side, no matter
what. Like I'm not the loneliest person in the world anymore. It
feels really fucking good.

Maybe it's the cool fall air, maybe it's the fact that we're
forming some sort of a plan. Maybe it's that—for once—it's just
the two of us.

All I know is I want to see her this happy as long as I'm alive.

25 ROSE

IT'S ODD, SEEING ABEL IN ANYTHING OTHER THAN HIS blue scrubs, faded and formless. It was even stranger seeing his naked body. I only caught a glimpse of his penis and if I wasn't mistaken, it was partially erect. I blush as I remember the sight of it. I turn to peek back at him, noticing his frown. It's almost painful, how beautiful he is—his skin a little flushed, his eyes narrowed a bit.

I wonder when we'll kiss again. Or when he'll teach my body to orgasm. These are the things I'm thinking as we get into the truck.

He takes the key and pushes it into the ignition and when the engine rumbles, he reaches for my face and kisses me.

There are no casual kisses between us, I'm convinced. Every kiss is like a message to my soul. As if Abel is wordlessly reminding me that he's a monster's miracle. Whether slow and tortuous or quick and hard, every kiss makes my heart tumble.

We stop and get gas and I stay in the truck. I watch as Abel takes the plastic bag filled with our old clothes and tosses it into the dumpster. Like that chapter of our lives is gone forever.

We're back on the road and I tell him where to head as my eyes start to droop. Several times, I jerk awake, expecting to be back in my bed at Silverwing. Every time, Abel squeezes my hand as if to tell me it's okay and that I can go to sleep.

But I don't because even though I'm thoroughly exhausted, I'm filled with a strange adrenaline that doesn't quite take off but sits in my abdomen. The way it buzzes is the only way I can tell it even exists.

After an hour, I fiddle with the radio and Abel smiles, his eyes still on the road. I'm wishing we were already there. I want his eyes and his hands and those lips. I want the things I didn't let myself dream of at Silverwing.

Hope is dangerous until you meet someone who can give it life, I suppose.

Abel drives confidently, just a little over the speed limit, sometimes more than a little when he seems to think he can get away with it. And he does because just as the tank starts to hit the empty zone, we're pulling into my old town. Part of me wants to press my nose against the glass and take in all the inevitable changes but a larger part of me knows I can't be seen so I remain in my seat, content to look at what I can in passing.

"Has it changed much?" Abel's voice cuts through my weary worries.

And I nod. "Life went on without me," I whisper.

"Shit, I don't know if mine would."

He's frowning a little when I look over and I risk not seeing all the changes just to stare at him. I direct him all the way to my mother's neighborhood.

My house doesn't look as formidable as it did in my dreams. It's just another large house with brown siding and a long driveway. It sits on top of the hill, far enough away from the end of the cul-de-sac to give my mother the privacy she required but with a neighborly touch. A woman full of contradictions.

"So, what's the plan?" He asks as he parks the car outside the driveway. "If she's in there, you can't kill her."

My brows are drawn before I know it. "If I wanted to, I would.

And you couldn't tell me otherwise." I don't like the way my chest pinches at the thought of Abel denying me what I've waited years for.

"No, I don't mean *ever*, baby. Just at a better time? When we're stable?"

That word makes me stop again. It's like that word has some kind of magic over me. *Does Abel know that? Is he saying it so I'll react calmly? Does he know he's my weakness?*

Baby. That word makes any annoyance I might've had pause and ebb. His eyes sparkle at his insistence; those beautiful blue eyes that his mother hated but I...*love.*

Love is frightening and so much bigger than I am. Perhaps it's my love that forces my nod. I know we'll never be in a better place. I know that if I see my mother inside, I'll kill her, but I don't tell Abel that because that might be what love does to me. It makes me want to lie to him to keep him happy—something I'd never done before.

I hate liars.

Love makes me a liar to keep him happy.

If he's happy, he won't leave me.

In my love, I'm frightened.

In my love, I'm a liar. For him.

"So, what's the plan, Rose?" he repeats, snapping me from my thoughts.

I blink a few times. "There's a safe inside. My father used to keep emergency cash in there. I don't know if my mother ever knew that safe existed."

It's like I can hear my father in my ear, telling me and my sister that he'd hid some money away in case we ever needed it. Had he known I'd meet my demise by my mother's lies? Had he known I'd be the one to take his life?

I try to shrug it off, but Abel's eyes are so direct. They're staring into my soul and I am shame. "I don't know." I try to say what I'm feeling but I don't know the words.

"Does thinking of him make you sad?"

I shake my head and blink away the moisture in my eyes. "No. It fuels my need to kill her."

Abel doesn't say anything else. It's time for me to go inside.

"I'll be back," I whisper, glancing around.

He stops my head from its turning, his palms against my jaw. *Heavy is the head*...it's so very nice to rest my head in his hands.

"You be careful."

"I will," I assure him. His eyes stare at me for a good while and I'm staring right back. "If I don't make it out..."

He presses his lips to mine before I can finish, and I sigh into his mouth.

I can't read his mind, but I can read his lips as they part against mine.

Make it back to me.

I pull away before I start to second guess myself. Without another word, I slide out of the car and run toward the first tree. I don't see anyone out, even in the foggy daylight that looks more gray than anything else. I rush the rest of the way, always looking around, ready to dive into hiding.

I make it to the front of the house with no problem. I don't stop because stopping could make me nostalgic and any emotion would weaken me right now.

Knowing my mother, she hasn't changed the locks, she hasn't removed the spare key from its place inside the lantern, and she hasn't changed a single thing in her life because she thinks I'm no longer a threat. She probably still has my father's last name and pretends to be a grieving widow, embarrassed by her insane daughter.

I reach inside the lantern and, sure enough, it's there. Her smugness infuriates me, but I inhale deeply before nodding at Abel. He remains in the car as I unlock the door and step inside.

Nothing has changed. Not a single thing is different, and it almost feels like I've stepped inside a time machine. The house is quiet, and I wonder if anyone is here. By the looks of it, I'm alone. But I remain quiet as I maneuver in the place I used to feel most safe in.

I pause in the kitchen and open one of the drawers—the drawer that I know holds the knives. I don't touch any of them, but I see it sitting there among the others like it's just another blade. It isn't. Sharpened and polished to perfection, this is the knife that I'll kill my mother with.

It has sentimental value, after all. Before I can delve into my memories, I push the drawer closed and move toward the steps.

I walk up the stairs as quickly as I can and can't help but glance in my sister Grace's room. Empty.

I'm torn between disappointment and relief. If she isn't home, there's a good chance my mother isn't either.

I head to my old room and expect the worst as I turn the knob.

All my things are boxed, and my bed is gone. This place should remind me of my halcyon days, when I wasn't another member of the cattle and before I'd taken my father's life; but all it does is remind me of how misplaced I was here. I wasn't quite *out* but I certainly wasn't *in*.

I rifle through my old things, grab a backpack, and stuff clothes and things inside it. My ears hear all types of creaks and groans throughout the house but every time I pause, there's only silence. I grab my backpack and head toward my mother's room.

My body feels warm and my vision is distorting. I can feel my violence taking over at the thought of being faced with her. But when I push her door open, her bed is empty and made. As I stand there, staring at the bed my father died in, the phone rings, making me jump. A few more rings and the answering machine picks up.

"Mrs. Montgomery, this is Dr. Joe Brown at Silverwing Mental Institution. It's come to our attention that your daughter and another patient have escaped early this morning. Due to her history of violent behavior, I thought it best to notify you. We're already searching, and you likely have nothing to worry about.

Without money, they hardly could've gotten far. If you do see her, I'd call the police…"

I press the button to silence the message as I sit on my mother's bed.

So, he wanted to warn her? How kind of him.

I reach over and press the "delete" button.

It's too late, Joe.

You can't stop karma. Not when she takes human form.

26 ABEL

WHAT THE FUCK DOES ONE DO WHILE THEIR GIRLFRIEND
is inside their childhood home, gathering reconnaissance to kill the
only living parent they have left?

I've played with the radio. I've driven up and down the block.
This place looks empty. No people. Not even any fucking dogs.

Who doesn't own dogs?

There isn't any sign of anyone coming or going but my palms
still sweat.

I have a feeling I'll be wiping them on my pants until I have
Rose next to me again.

27 ROSE

GETTING INTO THE SAFE WAS EASIER THAN I HOPED. IT was hidden under my father's desk in his office and by the looks of it, no one had been in there in years. Dust was settled over what wasn't covered.

All I had to do, I muse as I head toward the truck as stealthily as possible, was push a few boxes around the closet in his office, lift the floorboards, and enter the code he'd given.

My birthday.

10151999.

Abel would ask how I felt about that.

I didn't feel a thing.

There was a hundred thousand dollars in there, all crisp hundred-dollar bills—now stowed in my backpack. There was also a gun in there, which I swiped quickly.

"Hey," Abel says as I climb inside. "How'd it go?" He's looking me over, eyes perusing my face and hands and body like he's making sure I'm in one piece.

"I was thinking of a change in scenery," I start before reaching in my pocket and pulling out a key. "My dad's old Porsche is still in the garage."

He frowns. "I don't know. I like this truck. We blend in."

"The truck is pretty loud. Besides, what happens when it breaks down? If we're attempting to get as far away from here as possible, we need a more reliable car."

"But then she'll know we were here."

"She'll know regardless. Joe called and left a message. I deleted it but I'm sure he'll call again."

Abel hits the steering wheel.

"Still, no one was home. And I have no idea when she'll decide to show up again."

Abel reaches across and grabs my face, and I let him, loving his grip on my chin. "We'll take the car then. Just get it and follow me. We'll get rid of this truck and hit the road."

"Just...don't forget what I want."

It's strange to have to include someone in my plans. It's the oddest thing, having to look in his eyes and tell him not to forget that I want to kill my mother in so many words. It's even stranger that he only nods and leans forward, rubbing my lips with his thumb.

And then a man is kissing his monster like her lips are carved from an angel.

28 ABEL

I WATCH ROSE AS SHE GETS OUT OF THE CAR, HER FULL backpack slung over her one shoulder. I didn't even think to ask her what the hell was in that thing. She looks back at me with a sweet smile and I want to tell her to hurry up before our luck changes, but I can't get over the way her hair shines under the sun that's peeking through the clouds, the golden strands that make her look like a *shikse* goddess.

Ma would slap the shit out of me if she could see me now.

I start the car and idle, waiting for her to pull out of the garage. I stare at the house as I wait. It's fucking huge. I've never been inside a house that looks as perfect as this one does. It looks like Rose should've had a better life than the one she was given.

It looked like she had a lot in common with this fucking house —beautiful on the outside but full of terrors on the inside.

A moment after the thought fades, I see her pull out of the garage. The car is silver, which is better than the red I'd expected when I heard her say *Porsche*. She pulls up beside me and shoots me a big grin. The biggest I've ever seen her wear.

She's radiant.

"Try to keep up," she yells before taking off. She isn't careful. She's excitement, and her fucking age for once.

I follow her through the streets even though it was supposed to be the other way around, my hands tightening on the steering wheel when she takes corners too sharply and goes over the speed limit. She parks the car just outside a shitty looking supermarket. I get out of the car and leave the key on the front seat. As far as I'm concerned, anyone can have that piece of shit truck. If they take it, better for us.

She's out of the car and leaning against the driver's side door when I approach.

"I'll bet you didn't come to this side of town often," I say before yanking her toward me for a kiss. I look down at her eyes. "No. This is where someone like me would be."

"Then I suppose I should've made an effort to venture this way." Her smile is cheeky as she swings her hair and gets in the passenger seat.

I rap my knuckles on the hood of the car with a grin on my face. Life is feeling *really* fucking good today. "You think you would've found someone like me, then?" I adjust the seat, messing with the buttons, not familiar with this type of car. If I were familiar, it'd only be in my goddamn dreams. *A Porsche?* Yeah. Never even been close enough to one to see my reflection.

"I'd say you're one in a million, but the earth's population is upwards of seven billion. So, I think you're one in seven billion, but that still doesn't seem completely accurate." She's unzipping her backpack as her words lose their volume until she's damn near murmuring to herself.

And I'm grinning like a fucking fool. "Whatcha got there?" I haven't moved the car anywhere, unsure what the hell we're doing next. The car purrs patiently as I see stacks of money peeking up at me. *Holy shit.*

"A hundred grand, some clothes, and a gun." She says these things casually like they're milk, eggs, and bread.

"Fuck. Let me see."

Her eyes slide up my face to my eyes as she pushes the bag toward me so I can look inside.

Sure enough, hundred-dollar bills, neatly bound, a gun, expensive by the look of it, and some fabric with flowers on it.

"We did it." The words are out of my mouth before I can think of anything else. "We fucking made it."

She grabs the bag back and closes it. "We still have a few more matters to take care of before we leave for good."

I glance around the empty parking lot. "And you have no clue when she'll be home?"

Rose shakes her head, her blonde hair sliding, strand against strand, as I wait for her to tell me what the plan is now.

"So, you want to just stick around here and wait for her?"

The silence in the car feels worse than any silence I've ever sat in before.

One moment, I can taste my freedom. The next, I'm a slave to her condition.

So fucking close…

"We won't get caught," she says.

"Yeah but you don't fucking know that, Rose. You don't know that." I sit back and turn the car off. "What about what *I* want?"

"I thought I was what you wanted."

"Damn it, of course you are. But," I'm afraid to ask, "am I what you want? Or am I just the guy who broke you out? The one you'll end up leaving behind if I decide enough is enough?"

She doesn't speak for a moment.

And if I thought the silence before was the worst, I was dead fucking wrong.

I have a feeling this silence will haunt me forever.

"You're what I want, too," she tells me.

And I believe her words. I believe them so much that I hear the things she isn't fucking saying. That's how hard I'm listening to this girl. I'm hearing the shit she won't tell me.

I love you, but…
I need you, but…
I want you, but…
I love, need, and want this more.
Fuck.

I wonder if Rose knows how shitty being in this town feels for me. My eyes are constantly moving, trying to make sure no one sees her.

"What are we doing?" I ask her.

She pulls a wad of cash from the bag and hands me three hundred-dollar bills. "We need food. And whatever else you can think of."

My eyes go from the money she's still holding out for me to grab to the building in front of us. By now, the sun is out, and some cars have started hitting the road. This quiet town is about to become a whole lot louder once Rose is through.

"Everything all right?" She reaches her free hand toward my face and I nod.

Her touch is thrilling, and I'm lost in her green eyes.

"I love you, you know. I wouldn't be here, wouldn't have gotten us outta that shit hole, if I didn't."

She lets me lean forward, so close to her lips that I'm nearly kissing her, before she responds. "You're not afraid of me. Not you too, Abel."

I close my eyes as my lips touch hers. So fucking softly that I don't know if I could even call this a kiss. "Not the way you think," I tell her again, because it's true.

I don't think my *basherte* will hurt me. But I know she's capable of hurting me indirectly and landing us both right back in Silverwing. Or worse, dead.

I don't want to die today. Or any time soon.

Certainly not before I have a chance to make her come.

I grin and lean back as I grab the cash. "Any requests?"

She shrugs. "As long as it isn't oatmeal."

I get out of the car and head toward the entrance. My eyes are still doing that shifty thing because I'm a shitty criminal. Luckily, I'm the only customer inside.

I grab socks, underwear, t-shirts, body wash, and a shitload of snacks. When I see condoms, I shove three boxes into the basket. Her pleasure, because I'm a gentleman. I grab two disposable phones and as I make my way toward the register, I see sunglasses. I take two pairs and drop them into the almost-full basket.

There are bins full of promotional items in the front of the store. It's full of Halloween decorations and I grin as I look through it. I used to love Halloween. Ma would say it was an evil holiday. That no matter what people dressed as, *a nar bleybt a nar.* A fool remains a fool.

I see something at the bottom of the bin and tuck it into my basket.

The music over the speaker makes me think of elevators as I approach the only register with a person behind it.

"Morning," the young woman says.

And I nod as I look around the register at the mints and gum and candy.

She rings the items up and offers idle chit chat but I'm not here for that shit.

It's weird, how friendly she is. There'll be a day when people will know we escaped. They'll call us savages and say all kinds of crazy shit about us but this girl, the one I smile at before handing her one of my bills, I think about what she'd say.

Would she say she was afraid? Would she lie?

I grab the bags and tell her to have a good day.

I hope they get that on fucking camera.

As I leave the store, I look at the surveillance camera just above the door and wave.

Because I'm a nice fucking guy.

29 ROSE

I INSISTED WE DRIVE FORTY-FIVE MINUTES OUT OF town. I've never been in this area, but Abel pulled into the first motel parking lot.

He's inside getting a room situated and I'm sitting in the car, truly embracing my freedom as I chew on a licorice stick he purchased at the store. I glance at the bags he tucked behind the driver's seat with curiosity. He claimed he didn't want me peeking, as if there was something in there that I shouldn't see. Did he not realize that telling me not to do something made me want to do it even more?

I think back to the things Joe said. About the way I react to authority.

Directions make me itch to lash out.

But when Abel told me not to look in the bags, I didn't want to hurt him. I didn't want to punish him.

I simply wanted to defy him.

I'm about to reach in the backseat when he pushes the door open and steps outside. I have to press my thighs at the sight of him; the way the autumn breeze catches the ends of his brown hair, which looks so much lighter in the sunlight. I'm oddly awed by the smoothness of his gait. The paleness of his complexion. The way his body looks so thin, but I know, the sinewy muscles, the sprinkle of hair, the strength when he holds me. One look at Abel and I don't think of sex as just another human function and the trading of disgusting fluids one wouldn't otherwise touch.

I think of touching and more kissing and a deep-seated lust that I never knew existed.

He opens the car door and slides inside. "Got us a nice little room," he says, holding up the keys with a salacious grin.

On others, it would disturb me. On him, it makes me arch my brow and turn away for fear of embarrassing myself.

And then he has the decency to ask me if I'm okay.

"Of course. Why?" I'm still staring out the window.

"Your face looks a little pink and you won't look at me."

He touches my jaw and I close my eyes before turning my face toward where he's sitting.

"Open your eyes, *basherte*."

I do, and he has this stoic and serious expression like he's carved from stone. But if I were to touch him now, I'd prove that thought wrong.

Soft skin, easy enough to slice through; hardly any flesh, nothing to resist a blade, really.

I bet his blood would look beautiful against his skin.

But if the universe knows anything at all, it knows that the day Abel bleeds is the day everyone does.

I blink and Abel smiles.

"Atta girl." He presses a kiss to my lips and starts the car.

We aren't too far from the office, but he insists we should have the car as close to our room as possible. I hear what he isn't saying. *In case we need to run.*

I'd be afraid. I'd be terrified.

But I wouldn't be running alone and that keeps me from any of those uncharacteristic emotions.

· · ·

THE WATER PRESSURE in this motel room is terrible. For the lack of hot water at Silverwing, at least the water pressure was enough to cause pain at times. It's the opposite here and I wonder if life will ever grant me access to the perfect shower again. I would give anything to shower at my old house. The shower heads made me a believer of magic, I think to myself as I lather up and wash the hours of freedom from my pores. The hours of uninterrupted time with Abel.

As soon as we entered the room, Abel put on a fresh shirt and handed me a few things from one of the mysterious plastic bags and suggested I take a shower and relax for the rest of the day. I suspect I'll know the bags' contents soon enough. The knobs squeak as I turn off the water and the steam feels lovely settling on my now pink skin.

The towels are soft enough. They certainly do an adequate job of drying me.

My backpack full of clothes is sitting on the toilet but, as I stand here naked, I decide I don't want to wear any of the perfect clothes my not-so-perfect mother picked out for me. I grab the shirt Abel had taken off and I put it on. I bring the collar to my nose and sniff it with a smile. I'm tempted to walk out of this room naked, but the moment those bright blue eyes look at me, I'd fumble and falter and that's a situation I could easily do without.

I rifle through the bag of perfect clothes and grab a pair of underwear. Thankfully, I won't be forced to wear plain cotton underwear again. My mother wanted my underwear as perfect as my clothes.

I pick up a red lace pair and I wonder if my mother wished me more brazen.

Maybe she thought sex would help.

Maybe I did, too. Maybe that's why I offered my body to boys I didn't care for.

It's dangerous to implant this idea in a young woman's mind, that she could need fixing and that she may find repair in the hands of boys.

Any one of them could've been killed, had they broken my heart.

Thankfully—in spite of what had been hoped for me—I was never that invested. And they were safe.

I twist the doorknob I'd left unlocked. A small part of me wishes Abel had found the courage to join me in my shower. But the fumbling and faltering would commence so perhaps it was best he hadn't.

As soon as I step over the threshold into the room, I see lights. Colorful Christmas lights strung and hanging from the two lamps on the opposite sides of the bed. It looks as though any breeze could destroy the display he'd worked on but…it's beautiful.

My eyes are wide, and he stands just a foot from the edge of the bed, arms loosely at his sides.

"Abel." It's all I can say, really.

"I just want this time to be about us," he says as he takes me by the hand.

My skin still feels a little clammy from the shower and I don't want to be nervous. Not about the fact that I'm only wearing panties and his t-shirt. It wasn't the cleanest thing to don but I feel a little saner when surrounded by his scent. Less like a woman hanging from a ledge with three fingers keeping her from falling to her death. Or the death of the world around us.

"Everything is about us," I tell him, hoping in earnest that he believes me.

He tugs me a little and I follow him down until I'm sinking and then lying on the mattress. The Christmas lights create a haze of color that make this handsome boy look like a dream. Abel's bright eyes still shine as I lie beside him.

He reaches a hand to cup my face and I scoot a little closer.

"It's like I went through life not thinking to want because I couldn't put exactly what I wanted into a specific idea or, I don't know," he said. "Ma would say I've got the *shpilkes*. I was restless and that's why I didn't date, and I was fucking hopeless. I still don't know if I really believe in soul mates or *basherte* but, who do I thank for knowing exactly what I needed and bringing you to me?"

His words make me breathless. I suppose hearing the right words make it so you don't have to say a single thing in return.

He rolls on top of me and takes my face in his hands. He's supporting his weight on his elbows and knees, but I still feel flustered by his nearness. This is so unlike any other physical exchange I've taken part in. Abel is a torch and I am gasoline, and together we are a massive explosion.

"I bought condoms," he tells me, his eyes dancing between my own. "If you're ready."

"I shouldn't be afraid…"

He shakes his head and kisses me once, gently.

I lift my feet and place them outside his knees. My legs are spread and my knees are bent, and when he dips down to kiss me, I run my fingers through his hair. His hand slides from my knee to my thigh before wedging between the mattress and my hip. He lifts me, so I'm right in line with his erection and I bite down on his bottom lip at the sweet ecstasy of it.

He moves us closer to the headboard and when I sink back into the mattress, I scramble to remove the shirt he's wearing. He presses me back into the pillows and sits up. There's something about the slow slide of his shirt against his abdomen that makes me dizzy. His pale skin, the dark smatter of hair below his navel, the way his eyes watch me watch him.

"What do you want, *basherte*? What do you need, *sheyn royz*?" he asks as he lowers back against my waiting body.

"I'm not sure." *Are there words for what I'm feeling?* "I don't know how to put what I feel into words."

I don't crave that control.

He can have it.

He runs the tip of his tongue over my neck, up toward my jaw and back down to my collarbone, and I dig my nails into his arms.

"What...I don't..." I close my eyes and swallow.

"Shhh," he tells me as he sits up again and slides his hands under the white t-shirt that once looked so right as it hung from his body; the one that now covers mine. "Your mouth doesn't work because your body's taking over. And that's okay, Rose." His hands are just under my breasts, resting at my ribs for just a moment. "That's more than okay."

When he sweeps a thumb over my nipple, I feel the oddest sensation. Sneaky lust climbs into my navel and slides right down to my toes.

"You don't want me to be scared of you, but I think if I let go, you'll be scared of me," he whispers. "So, I'll take it slow even though I'm dying to push myself inside of you. Right..." he presses the heel of his hand into me, where my panties cover me, and I groan, "...here."

I lift my lids and Abel's gaze on my body makes me dig my toes into the bunched-up comforter. One of his hands caresses my bent knee, like he's afraid I'll move. The other has my shirt lifted over my breast.

If there were any healing hands, they'd belong to Abel.

He's leaning down and I slide my free leg down with impatience.

His mouth is already partially open and he's descending to my breast.

And then an alarm shrills, causing him to jerk up at the same time I do. My teeth hit his chin and I can taste the coppery tang of his blood just before he sits up and scrambles toward the door. I tug down my shirt and rush after him. He's already out the door and rushing down the steps toward the Porsche, its lights blinking. I run back inside and grab the keys to turn the wretched sound of the alarm off. When I look out, I see Abel turning around and around, as if to see who'd caused the ruckus.

I press the button and turn the alarm off. In the quiet, I realize just how barren this place is.

Abel looks up at me, his mouth open to speak, his shoulders raised in confusion, when someone jumps out from the bushes and tackles him.

30 ABEL

I DIDN'T SEE THE GUY JUMP ME UNTIL IT WAS TOO LATE.
Now the fucker is wrestling me to the ground because my defenses
were lowered.

The kid who used to get his ass kicked by bullies takes a
moment to catch up. I've somehow ended up under this guy, taking
punches. I reach up and shove my hand into his Adam's apple
which makes him clutch at his neck. Just as I'm about to push him
off me, I see a fist come into view.

Rose, with the key between her knuckles, hits him in the cheek.
Now the guy's face is fucking leaking and I'm trying to get him off
me before I'm covered in the shit. Rose grabs him by his greasy
looking hair and proceeds to punch him over and over until I'm up
from under him and pull her away by her waist.

"You're gonna kill him," I ground out as she fights me.

She goes limp in my arms and as I look down, I see we're both
wearing this guy's blood.

He's not moving, and I'm scared as shit to check his pulse. He
might not be as lucky as the last guy Rose attacked.

"I was aiming to kill him," Rose tells me, her words full of
determination even if she's out of breath.

He looks homeless, from his dirty clothes to the stench coming off his body.

I turn her around and look her in the eye.

Mishegas. I hear the word my ma would say like a whisper in my ear.

A couple blinks and I'm focused on Rose again. "I need you to go upstairs and lock the door. I'll be back. Only open the door for me." I glance at the guy lying on the pavement, his hair covering his eyes.

"How will I know it's you?" she asks, not bothering to wipe away the blood on her skin. Like she loves the shit there, wearing it proudly like some fucked up kind of trophy.

I just need her to move. "Go, *basherte.*"

This feels surreal as I kiss her forehead and she walks up the stairs. It's then that I notice she's still only in my t-shirt and her underwear.

Still, when she turns to look at me before shutting the door, she looks like my Rose. Like the same girl I saved. The one who saved me.

It trips me the fuck out as I grab this guy by his ankles and drag him toward the dumpster. I check his pulse and its faint but he's still alive. I grab his arm and fireman lift him into the dumpster. It wasn't like this asshole wasn't asking for a beating.

But I bet he wasn't expecting to get his ass beat by Rose.

Being homeless was a fight to stay alive. Mother Nature, other people, it wasn't easy. But never in my homelessness, had I ever tried to break into someone's car or attack someone for a fucking payday.

This car is too nice for this area. We're attracting too much attention.

Time to go.

Walking back to the room, I feel less alone than I'd like to. I catch someone on the lower level peeking through their curtains, but I don't bother wiping away the blood on my body. When I lift my hand to wave, they move away from their curtains and I know it's time for me and Rose to move the hell on and fast.

I think about this person and what they'll say when the media comes knocking.

They'll say that Rose and I attacked a man, unprovoked. They'll say I then threatened them.

And sure, I think the worst of people. Sure, they might not call the cops and they might not say anything when the cameras come.

But I've learned that nine times out of ten, people take the shittiest routes.

Fuck people.

It's me and Rose against the motherfucking world.

Them versus us.

And we'd win.

We fucking have to.

31 ROSE

"YOU'RE NOTHING MORE THAN A FUNCTIONING psychopath."

Words aimed to hurt only slid from my ear drums like the waste that they were.

"And you're nothing more than an evil woman, pretending to be someone's salvation," I said.

"You make me sound like some sort of god," she responded with a chuckle, her bloody hand leaving a smear on her cheek as she tried to push her hair away from her face.

Oh, mother. You never were perfectly put together. For once, you appeared as maniacal on the outside as you are in your very core.

"A god? One with power over human fortunes and human life? One revered as the almighty being in control?" I grunted over the pain lancing through my back. The sight of her with my blood on her hand and on the knife she was holding enraged me. But I heard the sirens, I knew they were coming. "There are no gods here. Though if there were one, I'm certain you wouldn't be the primary candidate for the title."

. . .

A LOUD BANG snags my attention, pulling me away from my sightless gaze aimed at my bloody fingers.

Wordlessly, Abel leads me to the bathroom and washes my hands gently, pressing a kiss to each knuckle.

Is this gratitude?

"Let's pack," he tells me, urgency dripping in his tone.

And in my nostalgic melancholy, I acquiesce.

32 | ABEL

IT DOESN'T TAKE US LONG TO PACK ALL OUR SHIT UP. WE
don't even check out, just drop the bloodied keys on the bed and
leave. I'd paid cash for the night. They could keep the change.

We're driving back toward Rose's hometown and then past it
for another half hour. I wish I could push the gas to the fucking
floor and be rid of this godforsaken place. If Ma were here, she'd
beat my ass.

*Leave that shikse. You're a good boy. All that mishegas isn't good for you,
Abel.*

But what the fuck did Ma know?

She died holding an empty beer can with vomit in her throat.

We pull into another motel and I make Rose wait in the car
again as I get us situated. By the time I reach the car with a new set
of keys in hand, I see Rose fast asleep through the window. I grab
the backpack and sling it over my shoulder before grabbing our
bags of snacks and shit and reaching for her. She stirs but I take her
in my arms and carry her toward our room. She isn't heavy but I'm
thankful we're on the ground floor because I'm tired as fuck.

I unlock the door and place her on the bed before going into the
bathroom and rinsing my face off. I'd cleaned up after the fight, but

I could still hear the sound of Rose's fist hitting the guy's face, and the keys between her knuckles puncturing it. I drag my tired ass to the bed and turn on the television, flipping it to the news. After a half hour, I start to relax. We aren't on the news.

Yet.

I look down at Rose as she sleeps, and I smile.

To have seen her at her worst, hands bloodied and ruined by solitary...

I grab one of her hands and the bruised knuckles make me frown.

I kiss each one of them and turn over to face her.

Scary as shit to think I hadn't seen anything yet but I don't think I've witnessed her worst. Not yet, anyway.

My life is full of that fucking word. *Yet.* I try not to wonder about the future, but I can't even help that shit.

What kind of future do Rose and I have to look forward to? One where we're always looking over our shoulders? What could we really fucking do?

We couldn't have a normal life.

So, the question is, was it worth it? Was it worth taking her out of one hell to place her in a different one?

Was it worth offering her a life I didn't know I could really deliver?

What about me? I'd always wanted to buy a house, get married, and have a couple of kids. What about *my* future?

Rose isn't on medication and refuses to be helped and because I love her, I want her to be happy. But now that I have to worry about how deep I'm in and how entwined our lives are, I'm breathless. My chest hurts.

I rub my hand over my heart and sit up.

One of the phones is in the pocket of my pants. I reach into it, and pull it out, flipping it open and shut. Open and shut.

There's only one contact in this phone; the number of the second phone I'd purchased.

Because who the hell else would I have to call in my new life?

Only me and her.

Would that be enough?

I wonder...

But you love her, man.

I look down at her and I know I do. I love the parts that no one sees. I love the fucking hopes and dreams I see in her eyes. I don't regret saving her. I don't.

But I regret not thinking things through, not offering a way to make her take her medication.

I loved her selfishly instead. I didn't do right by her and now people will suffer.

Including me.

But fuck it.

I deserve it.

33 ROSE

ABEL'S LIMBS HOLD ME AGAINST HIM IN A MAKESHIFT prison.

But I don't count the seconds. Only his deep, loud breaths as they pass over my skin.

One, two, three...

His mouth is against the back of my neck, warming it, making me smile.

In Silverwing, I never bothered to hope for this. So, I revel in it.

A snore cuts through the room, disturbing the silence and making me jump.

Who knew such a beautiful person could make such terrible noises?

I slide from beneath his arm, my body crookedly angled as I try to figure out the best way to remove my legs from under his.

His snores are getting louder and louder and I decide to just slide off the bed quickly, nearly waking him. But, still, he sleeps. I peek through the curtains, sighing at the sight of the gray sky only broken up by the streetlights lining the road. The world feels so empty.

There's one person the world needs to be rid of, I think to myself as I stare back at Abel.

The need gnaws at me, a beast in my own belly. I yearn for patience, assuring myself that I will have my time, and that Abel will make this a priority.

I tell myself all this as he continues to snore, each grumbly inhale and exaggerated exhale mocking my inner turmoil.

He grunts in his sleep and I tiptoe around the room, grabbing a sweater and jeans from the chair. Everything sounds so loud as I try to get ready as quietly as possible. When I'm dressed, I realize I don't have the keys. I tiptoe back toward my bag and when I look up to check if Abel's still sleeping, I see them on the nightstand, inches from his face.

My lips twist as I reach toward the keys. When he starts in on a loud snore, I jump a little and decide to snatch the keys and move quickly. Before I turn to leave, I see the gun beside the lamp and grab that as well. Then, I tuck it into my waistband and walk out of the motel room.

The morning air is foggy, and I pull my sweater closer to my body as I approach the car. The lack of sunlight causes me to glance around the empty parking lot and back up toward our room. No sign of Abel waking up, no sign of anyone else's eyes on me.

I climb in the car and turn it on. I try to ignore the way the gun in my waistband digs into my skin. Small price to pay for the release I'm looking forward to.

A little pain for a lot of pleasure.

Luckily, I remember the roads we took to get here.

No music, nothing but me and the open road. Part of me wishes Dr. Brown could see me now, in my Dr. Jekyll life.

Maybe he'd be proud.

But I know better than to even delve that far into such an unlikely situation.

He'd see the cracks in my mask, the one I let slip a few times already.

He'd see the flaws in our plans and insist I come back to Silverwing.

But he doesn't know anything.

Abel saved me.

I'm never going back.

I'm driving down the back roads when I hear something ringing. I open the glove compartment and see a phone. It looks cheap and disposable. I flip it open, press the green button, then the speaker button, and listen.

The connection crackles for a moment.

"Rose?" His voice sounds sleepy and worried.

And all at once, I wish I was there, next to him, basking in his warmth. Snores or not.

"Where are you?" he asks me.

I hesitate. Another crack in my mask. "I'm headed to my mother's."

"Rose," he groans. "Don't you think she'll notice the car you're driving? She'll notice that it's parked outside her house, not in the garage where she left it."

I question my genius, because I know I don't exercise it when it comes to my violence. I move without question. And I pay for it later. "I'll be fine," I assure him and he's quiet for a moment.

"But we're a team now. If you're gonna do anything, you have to tell me. Not because you need my permission but because my life is attached to yours. We rely on each other. I can't do this without you."

His words make me want to pull over and vomit. Too many emotions are battling one another and I'm in the middle, trying to decide which way to go. Abel's hand is stretched out toward me, willing me to cross to the other side, with him.

And my beast, my Mr. Hyde, runs his tongue over bloody teeth, promising the sweet release I *need*.

But as I pull to the side of the road, and rest my head on the steering wheel, I try to find words instead. "Are we? Really?" I look at the phone in my lap, as if he's going to somehow reach through the phone and reassure me with a touch.

"Do I have to bust us out of another psych ward to prove it?" he asks.

I hear the laughter in his voice and it makes me smile. "I'm not used to this," I tell him before picking my head up, just in time to see a police cruiser slow and pull up just behind the car.

"Abel," I start, my voice wavering, "a police officer just pulled up behind me." I hear nothing. But the beast inside causes me to clutch the steering wheel.

"Rose..."

"He just turned on his lights."

I won't make it out of this alive.

No.

He won't make it out of this alive.

Abel swears, and I can hear him rustling through something. "How long have you been driving? In what direction?"

I take a deep breath. "Probably a half hour toward h-home." Panic has me faltering, calling hell "home".

"Don't..."

"What if he recognizes me?" I ask, cutting him off.

"Baby..."

"I don't want to kill a police officer," I whisper.

I don't want to only be a monster.

I want to be a woman Abel could love.

Abel doesn't have anything to say to that as the man in uniform raps on my window, my wide eyes reflected in his black shades.

34 ABEL

IF I EVER QUESTIONED MY LOVE FOR ROSE, I'D KNOW, IN this moment, that I was a fucking idiot.

There's nothing like wishing you could rescue the woman you love to really put your feelings in perspective. I'm holding the phone to my ear as I pull on clothes, grab a wad of cash, and head out of the room toward the front office.

"Everything okay, officer?"

Rose's voice comes through the phone and I place my hand over the mouth piece.

"Hey. Got a car I can borrow?" I ask the girl at the front desk.

She looks over at me and shakes her head.

I shove my hands in my pocket and pull out a wad of cash. "Let's try again. I have hundreds of dollars here. If you let me use your car for an hour, you can keep it."

She fishes in her purse and tosses me a set of keys. "It's the black Ford F-150 near the door."

I'm out the door at the tail end of her sentence and I press the phone into my ear, trying to hear Rose and the cop.

"I actually don't have my license on me and this is my father's car," Rose says.

She's losing the confidence in her words and I can't get to her fast enough.

I can't start the car fast enough. I can't peel out of the parking lot and rev down the road fast enough.

I'm not enough.

I don't know if I can save her this time.

"Please step out of the car, miss."

I don't hear anything for a moment, and then the officer asks her to step out again.

Do it. Dear God, do it, I think to myself. I've still got the phone pressed to my ear as I race toward my girl.

"Abel?" she whispers just before I hear movement on the other side of the line.

"Don't fight. Don't fight!" I yell as I press harder on the gas. The phone somehow disconnects, and I can only pray I'm heading in the right direction. The same direction we came from last night.

Fifteen minutes later, I see a cop car. The lights are still flashing, and the driver's door of the Porsche is ajar. I hop out of the truck, not sure if I'm ready to see whatever's gone on.

I hear someone breathing heavily and I rush toward the space between the cars.

Rose. Rocking back and forth. Her hands bloody, her eyes vacant.

The police officer. On the ground, blood staining the grass and rocks. I can't see where it's coming from, but I see the gun she stole from her mom a few feet from her.

"Baby?"

As soon as she hears me, her eyes snap right to me. She looks like a wounded little girl, her green eyes wide and looking at me like I'm supposed to fix this fucking mess. But for her, I would. Somehow, some fucking way, I'd fix it all for her.

"I didn't kill him, Abel. I'm sure I didn't." Her voice sounds sure, even though the sweet sound of it is a direct contradiction to the blood on her hands.

She's covered in the red shit and I don't know where it's coming from. *Is it from him? God help me, is it hers?* I reach down to feel for a pulse. *Fuck me, he's still alive.*

What the hell are we gonna do now?

"How'd you know?" I ask her as I reach for her hands, not giving a shit about the blood on them. But they make her skin slick, so I have to squeeze her fingers to keep my grip. She stands, using me for support. We both look down at him for a moment and then her breath hitches.

She's capable of this and yet, I can still look in her eyes and love her.

What the fuck does that make me?

"I can't kill someone who doesn't deserve it," she whispers, her lips hardly moving.

She looks up at me and I'm lost in her eyes, even as this fucking chaos rains down and around us. We're drowning in motherfucking chaos.

35 ROSE

ABEL IS PACING, MUMBLING TO HIMSELF. I WONDER IF the officer is bleeding out from the bullet I put in his stomach. I tried to aim where there were no vital organs, but you can never tell with these things.

"He isn't dead but that could change if we don't do anything," I say, finally coming to my senses.

Abel stops his pacing and looks at the officer. I try not to smile as he pinches his lips between his fingers because he's just so handsome, but I fail.

And when Abel looks at me, I worry he'll find my smile odd. This isn't the time to smile and yet when he's around, I can't help it.

"I have no idea what the fuck we're gonna do," he whispers.

Does he think I'm not capable of grasping the situation in its entirety? "We have to get rid of the patrol car. Afterward, call the emergency number and tell them there's an injured officer at this location. I don't know if he called this car in, so we'll need a new means of transportation." My brain is trying to sort out all the pieces in front of me and it's like my genius has finally returned.

Abel doesn't answer me about any of it. Instead, he whispers, "I hope to fucking God he doesn't have a dashcam."

He heads toward the driver's side of the cruiser and when he sticks his head inside, I nearly pray.

But religion and faith are for people who need something to blame when things go sour, as are destiny and fate.

"I don't see any cameras," he announces before sticking his head back in the vehicle.

Though, if there are such forces, they're smiling down on us now.

I grab the gun and stand, waiting for Abel to join me so we can figure out what we're going to do next. I'm putting the gun in my waistband when Abel approaches me.

"He probably called it in and gave them your license plate number. And he'll remember your face," he says as soon as he joins me, and I pause my securing of the weapon.

I glance past Abel at the officer on the ground.

I don't kill people who don't deserve it. But I *will* kill someone who threatens my freedom. My freedom with Abel.

I step around Abel and approach the man who happens to look like he's sleeping. He has no idea what's going on. If only he could remain in that blissfully unaware state.

But he won't. He'll wake up and he won't stop until I'm back at Silverwing. In my anxiousness, I am a fortune teller.

I tilt my head and close one eye before lifting the gun and flicking the safety switch.

A squeeze of the trigger and now we don't need to be afraid anymore.

I hear coughing behind me followed by spitting. I'm not afraid to do whatever I have to do to keep us together.

Don't you see what I do for us?

I want to ask Abel if he sees how much I love him. I want him to *know*, without a shadow of a doubt that this death was for us. I pulled the trigger with our love in my heart. I would kill anyone that threatens our future together. Anyone who hurts him. I'd kill anyone.

I'm tucking the gun in my waistband again when I look at Abel.

And it's like I'm right back at the beginning. I couldn't read him then. And I can't read him now, no matter how hard I try.

36 ABEL

WE'RE FUCKED.

I don't know what else to think as we get rid of the cop car. I wipe away as many fingerprints as I can, mindlessly. I try to ignore the phantom sound of the bullet piercing that poor officer's fucking skull.

I'm out of my goddamn mind. And if that's true, what's Rose? Everything I knew she would be. Everything Dr. Brown warned me about.

I'm a fucking idiot.

I drag the officer's body toward the car and lift him into the trunk. I tell Rose to go back to the motel room, but she doesn't. She stays and paces. And when she isn't pacing, she's staring at me. Like she's trying to figure out what's going on in my head.

But I have no fucking clue. All I know is this guy's fucking brains are looking back at me and I'm doing shit I never thought I was capable of doing.

"Follow me in the Porsche?" I ask her as I get in the cruiser.

She nods, and we drive for a little until I see the edge of what I think is a river. I drive around for a few minutes, trying to find the perfect place to dump the car. The Porsche inches behind me and I pull up to the lake's edge and hop out of the car.

"I need a big rock," I say as I start walking around. I never thought I'd be the kind of guy helping his girlfriend hide a dead body. A cop, at that. Sure, most cops were dicks, but he didn't deserve this shit. He was just doing his fucking job.

She calls me over and I see a huge ass rock. It takes a lot of sweat to get that son of a bitch to the car, but I do. I pop the trunk and part of me expects this guy to be up and ready to kick my ass, but he just looks like he's sleeping—despite the hole in his head— as I take off his shirt. It's a struggle and when Rose tries to help me I tell her to just wait in the car. I close the trunk and start wiping everything I touched and once I'm done, I put the car in drive. I drop the heavy ass rock onto the gas and jump back as it takes off into the water.

The car isn't submerged as it gets pulled down and Rose points that out.

"They're gonna find that car regardless. This just bought us some time," I inform her.

I'm not some poor *schmuck* looking for luck. I know luck doesn't favor my kind. I just want Rose to get it in her head that we have to get the fuck out of here.

She takes me back to the truck and when I get out, she does too.

"I'm just glad no one saw any of this." I look out at the road and shake my head. *Luck?* Yeah right.

As we get ready to head back, I press a kiss to her temple.

Mishegas. I can hear Ma saying it now.

"You take the Porsche to the motel," I tell her. "I'll follow."

Everything feels so different as I get in the truck and head back. I watch the dead town around me, wondering if anyone has any idea what the fuck just happened. Does Rose even know?

Does she know I'm freaked the hell out? I don't think I can

handle seeing someone else's brains leak from a hole in their fucking head.

We pull up and I park beside her. "I have to return the keys. Be up in a second."

"I think I need a nap," she whispers.

And I nod. Before I walk away, she grabs my hand and kisses my knuckles. Those green eyes are as beautiful as I remember, as fucking gorgeous as always.

"I love you, you know," she says against them.

The words are a straight shot to my heart and I can't help my smile. "I know," I tell her, and she heads to the room, a lightness in her step.

I almost feel like some normal guy when I walk away.

I give the lady at the front desk her keys and ask if there's a computer or something where I can look up a number. She says there isn't, but that I can look on her phone if I want. So I do.

With each letter I type in the search engine, it feels like I'm some chump who made promises I couldn't keep.

Joe...Brown...Silverwing...Psychiatrist.

A few articles come up but then I see a contact number. I grab one of the hotel pens and write the phone number on the inside of my forearm.

I give the girl her phone back and head upstairs. When I open the door, I see that Rose is sleeping so I try to keep quiet and tiptoe into the bathroom. I turn to look back at her and it's crazy how peaceful and beautiful she looks now. Her lips are parted a little, just a little, and her hair is all over the place. She sleeps like she knows I'm looking at her.

She looks like everything I'm not.

But I can't get it out of my head, the way the cop's body jerked as she shot him.

I lean over the sink as it plays over and over in my head. I gag and spit and gag one more time.

I stare at the sink, talking myself in and out of calling him. I'm in way over my goddamn head.

But I love her.

But can I do this?

But how will I survive without her?

But she'll kill everyone.

But she'll kill her fucking self!

I fucking can't...

My hands are shaking as I dial the number written on my skin. It rings once, and I lose my nerve, hanging up before he can answer. I shove my phone back in my pocket and scrub the number from my skin until I can't see it anymore.

Fuck.

I can't do this to Rose.

Whatever hell she belongs in, I'll be right in there with her.

We'll burn together.

We belong together.

I splash some water over my eyes and step back. I look paler than usual. My eyes look a little dead and it freaks me the fuck out.

I step out of the bathroom to see her sitting up and rubbing the sleep from her eyes.

"Hello, Abel," she says as she tugs the sheets from her body.

When she walks up to me, I kiss her forehead and hug her close to my body. "I love you, you know."

Her fingers dig into me a little and I shut my eyes for a second.

She pulls back and looks at me, her eyes clear and wide.

How can she look this angelic when she's capable of such evil things?

How can I love her when she makes me question my own goddamn humanity?

"I know," she says before stepping out of my arms and walking into the bathroom.

. . .

THE NEXT MORNING, Rose is already awake when I finally open my eyes.

"It's about time, Mr. Sommerfeldt," she teases me as she turns off the TV and rolls over on her side to look at me. "I thought you might be dead but your snoring kept me from worrying."

I rub my eyes because I don't want her to see the shit going on in my mind.

I stayed up late because I was afraid I'd have a fucking nightmare about that goddamn cop she killed. The same one I fucking dumped in the river.

What. The. Fuck.

What the fuck are we doing?

I grab her hand and kiss her wrist before getting up and heading to the bathroom to brush my teeth and piss. I don't look at my reflection. I'm too disgusted with myself right now to even look myself in the eye. I feel like I don't know what the fuck we're gonna do and I *hate* it. I hate that I can't keep Rose safe, away from people. I hate that she won't let me and I *fucking* hate that she's so goddamn adamant with this stupid ass list.

I hit the counter with the palm of my hand and brace myself over it.

"Fucking hell," I say under my breath as I turn off the water.

When I leave the bathroom, Rose is gathering some things.

"What are you up to?" I ask before clearing my throat. I feel like shit.

"Getting ready so we can see if my mother is home yet."

Fuck.

I'm quiet as she goes through bags and shit but before she goes into the bathroom, I feel like I have to talk to her. "We need to get out of here."

She stops. "What are you talking about?"

"You'll have to handle your business soon or we'll have to skip town and come back this way when things have died down."

"We aren't even on the news, Abel. I watched the news all morning. We're completely fine."

"You killed a cop, Rose. Shit like that doesn't just go unnoticed."

"There are no witnesses."

I'm trying not to lose my patience, but she can't be fucking serious. "There is no way we're getting away with this. We were as careful as we could be, but shit like this doesn't just go unnoticed. Things aren't fine just because you don't know how shit works!"

Her eyes squint a little and she takes a second before she answers. "I always thought couples argued because they didn't quite like each other. I see I was wrong." She walks away and shuts herself in the bathroom.

I want to give her space, but I can't. I know what she's capable of. I've seen what she can do to people. I don't know if she'd do anything to hurt herself but it's a chance I won't take. I can hear the bathtub water running. I hesitate before doing anything; I try to listen, but I don't hear anything else.

I knock first and she doesn't answer, so I walk in.

She's naked and the tub is already halfway filled. There are no bubbles to cover her body from me.

"I don't particularly enjoy us being upset with each other," she says and there's this cute fucking pout on her face.

I imagine chains wrapped around the arms I cross over my chest, keeping me from rushing to her. She didn't ask me to come in and she sure as shit isn't asking me to fuck her. As badly as I want to. "I'm not upset with you, baby. I just need you to think outside the box because I guaran-fucking-tee the authorities are. You've dealt with them before. Those assholes will try to pin so much shit on us if we get caught. If we wanna avoid that, we have to be more careful."

"I don't often think about the way my decisions affect you. I'm sure that bothers you."

I nod my head but keep my arms crossed. "I'd like a little warning before I have to get rid of a fucking body."

"You witnessed your first murder. And what did you do? You hid the body." She twists her pretty pink lips.

"I didn't have much of a choice," I whisper, but it's a fucking lie. I could have turned her crazy ass in. I wasn't this person. I didn't do this kind of shit. But, man, I was so gone over this girl.

"Have I changed you, Abel? What would your ma think?"

She'd call you a shikse, spit on your face, and drag me away by my ear.

And you would fucking kill her.

I don't say a word as I approach her and sink to my knees. It's almost like I'm kneeling to my queen. Like I'm some goddamn servant and I should be kissing her royal ring or some shit. But I don't. Instead, I grab her by the back of her neck and kiss her lips with all the pent-up sexual tension in my body. She groans as our tongues dance and my fingers slide down her damp neck.

Her tongue tastes sweet, her saliva mixing with mine to make some sort of cocktail that I can't get enough of. I run the pad of my thumb over her nipple and she bites down on my tongue before pulling away.

I can taste the coppery tang of my blood as she stares at me with hooded eyes. I touch my finger to my tongue and when I pull it away, sure enough, there's blood.

"Do you want to touch me?" she asks.

And I nod even though what I really want to say is *fuck yeah.*

She sits up and leans into the edge of the tub to kiss me. Immediately, her tongue runs over my lips and I part them.

What. The. Fuck.

Her tongue is in my mouth and that coppery taste is mixing with the taste of us. I can feel her smile as she pulls away and I wonder if she just wanted to see what my blood tasted like.

Fucking twisted but my hard-on isn't going anywhere yet, not even when I see a tint of red coating her teeth.

She grabs my hand and places it between her breasts. I try not to be disappointed that I'm not touching her naked wet tits but I'm patient. All in due time.

She slides my hand down...down...down as she sits back and leans against the tub and spreads her legs.

Holy. Sweet. Shit. Fucking. Hell.

"I never let boys touch me here."

"I'm not a fucking boy," I whisper with force as my hand is slowly pushed under the warm water. "And I should be the *only* one touching you here."

"You are." Her breath hitches as I slide my fingers against her pussy, scissoring her lips and pressing them together so she cries out. "The only one."

"Want me to make you come?"

She shakes her head and I sit back a little.

Huh?

"I don't think I'm ready. I just, I wanted to see if you could make me feel good."

"Good? I can do you better than that."

She chuckles and it's husky. It makes me want to ignore her and press a finger inside. I look down at her and press my thumb against her clit. She grits her teeth and her hands clamp down over mine, stilling me.

"Too much," she whispers.

She doesn't know that's what coming is like. Too much. Too intense. Too out of motherfucking body.

I pull my hand away and she slumps back a little. "I'll leave you to it, then."

"Abel," she starts.

But I've already opened the door and walked out.

And right up against the door, I jack off, imagining the way she'll look when I *really* give her too much.

37 ROSE

MY BRAIN ISN'T WORKING EFFICIENTLY AS I REACH OVER to stop the water's flow. Instead, it's competing in what seems to be a losing game against my body. The goosebumps spreading over my exposed skin make me want to climb out and face whatever is on the opposite side of the door. *Is he here? Is he gone?* As soon as the water ceases to run, I'm reminded of my momentary cowardice.

I felt my heartbeat in my head, my throat a prison to the words I wouldn't offer. His touch, gliding across my skin at the pace I set, was as soft as I'd always hoped it would be.

He was the moment's master, and my unease was apparent in my lack of consent.

But now the moment's gone. He's gone. And I don't know what to make of the silence and the emptiness of this bathroom. The sight of the pale blue peeling linoleum is enough to make me long for a home I've never had and can only think fondly of from time to time. *Nonsensical thoughts.*

Abel is my first bit of true comfort. He's my home now.

It's so silent, I can easily remember the way my heartbeat sounded in my ears. The difference between the current silence and the previous cacophony makes me slow to inhale and afraid to exhale. The silence steals my breath. I'm trying so hard to hear a sound. Anything from the other side of the door.

Is he gone for good? Is that all it took?

In my lust, I am a coward and I will bear the brunt of that. In this tub, I am painfully lonely.

I hear something just outside the door, a quiet thud, and I sink back into the water, letting myself fall...fall...fall until I'm submerged.

I can hear my heart beating again as it thumps in my chest, keeping me alive.

My heart is a cruel creature, continuing to beat after I've stopped those in others.

My body is a cruel creature, wanting Abel more than words can say.

I sit up and inhale harshly, rushing air into my lungs before wiping the water away from my face.

I thought that in order to live, I had to protect my vital organs. My heart. My brain.

I could list them all with ease, but I couldn't lose one of them and survive. It was physically impossible.

And then I met Abel Sommerfeldt and he became something no one else has ever been.

Abel is a vital organ, living outside my body, and if I lose him, I would not survive it.

When I gather the courage to leave the bathroom, I breathe at the sight of Abel in bed, his face relaxed in resting.

A WHIMPER CRACKS through the dark room and immediately, I'm awake and aware, listening for another.

Something close to a gasp escapes from the person sleeping beside me. I stare into the darkness, waiting to hear anything else.

I clench my fists to keep from counting. Not with Abel. Not when I have nothing to worry about.

I prefer the mumbles and sighs more than the throaty sounds and deep snores.

Still, in my worry, I wonder.

In an attempt to keep from doing so, I turn onto my back and take a few deep breaths.

I've nearly found my way back into sleep when another sound jolts me back into consciousness.

He'd been quiet all day while we shopped for clothes and more food. I held back questions each time he sent me a small smile. Still, he remained quiet, even while watching television with his hand on some part of my body, like he knew I needed reassurance.

But his silence was likely of his own doing. Suffocating his thoughts, forcing them back inside until they had to come through as he slept. He shifts and settles, only to shift again, making those sounds again. Initially, it's just groans and grumbles of words I can't quite make out. I don't think much of it and I close my eyes again, relaxing back into sleep.

"Rose," he gasps.

I sit up and turn on the light on my side of the bed, scooting away from where he sleeps. As soon as the light is on, I peek over at him, unsure if he'd actually said it.

Is it me he's having bad dreams about? Is he finally afraid of me?

I can't see what he's thinking. His eyes are still shut and his jaw clenches as he dreams. He kicks his leg out and I scoot farther out of his way just as he says, "Don't kill him."

I still and peer over at him, this time knowing what I heard but not knowing how to react.

No.

I want to reach out and touch him, to claim him from the dream that's causing his fear of me. *He belongs to* me, *dream, not you.*

But it isn't the phantom that haunts his mind that did it. It's me: the outsider, the murderer, the mad mastermind.

I should have known it would be too much. That *I* am too much for him.

Foolish hope.

"No...he didn't deserve it."

He did, I want to scream. *He'd have taken us away from each other.*

Doesn't that frighten Abel the way it does me? How could he not see that I'd saved us?

The cop wasn't evil. But he became an obstacle that had to be vanquished.

Abel keeps his guilt quiet, his guard up, only to reveal his secrets to me when he is most vulnerable. Doesn't he know he can't hide from me?

He fists the sheets before shifting again. He shivers and I'm scrambling off the bed as quickly as I can, as if his remorse is contagious.

Whatever Abel's mind is putting him through, I don't want it.

"Don't do it," he says.

I can't be loved by a man like Abel.

In my resolve, I am on a mission, moving toward my final act. It was this, or me ending up facing the same life I'd only just run from. In a flurry, I'm searching, throwing clothes and shoes to find...

My hands touch it as I rifle through my backpack.

Cool metal, the feel of life's balance at your fingertips.

I'm no god. And no god could've planned, designed, and created me.

But I can feel some sort of holy duty, an unbearable and potent strength perched on my shoulders, threatening to crush me.

I'm no god but I have intimate knowledge on how profound it feels to steal a man's last breath.

My fingers wrap tighter around it and I aim at Abel. My hand shakes as my internal screams weaken me.

Wrong.

Wrong!

I bring the gun to my temple. I can feel my heartbeat in my hand and I blame my adrenaline.

Peace. Quiet.

Monster!

I don't want remorse. I don't want his remorse, and in his sleep, he tells me everything he would otherwise keep to himself.

My lids are pressed together as I tell myself I'm his nightmare. I am what is terrorizing him.

I am the monster in his life.

I switch the safety off.

Look at him. Don't do it without seeing him one last time.

When I open my eyes, Abel is staring at me.

"*Basherte?*"

How does he do this? How can he sit there, calm and expressionless when I'm all chaos, heartbreak, and confusion?

"You hate me," I whisper, and he shakes his head and moves toward me. With every inch that disappears between us, I loosen my hold on the gun.

"Never."

The words are more air than actual sound and it's like I can feel them as he scoots ever closer.

Never but...

"You wish I never killed him," I say.

He doesn't say anything, and I twist my lips as I adjust my grip on the gun. He eyes the movement and jumps off the bed to stand beside me. He doesn't try to grab the gun, he doesn't tell me to stop.

"Look." He grabs my free hand. "If you pull the trigger, you'll kill me, too."

Because you can't find life worth living if I'm no longer here? I finish his statement for him internally and slide the gun from my temple to my neck and all the way down until it's aimed at the floor.

I sob and lean against him as he reaches over to grab the gun from my flimsy grip.

"I'm your nightmare," I tell him.

I hear the click of the safety switch and the moment he drops the gun on the bed, he pulls me into his arms. I am filled with the peace I yearned for from a bullet the moment I'm surrounded by him.

In my panic, I am suicidal.

"What would I do without you?" he asks.

He's pressing kisses to my face, held between his hands, where tears run hot.

I dig my nails into his skin at my thoughts before settling on one. "Find a good Jewish girl who could never love you as much as I do."

"Fuck that shit." He pulls back to give me his icy blue eyes. "Don't wish that on me."

The left side of his lips stretch up and he lifts me right along with it.

He smiles like he didn't just catch me with a gun to my head and I'm wondering what kind of magic this man is.

"Do I scare you?" I ask the man who'd only just had a nightmare about me.

"Losing you scares me." He presses a kiss to my forehead, still attempting to soothe me. "That's about the one thing that could really fuck me up. You don't want that for me, do you?"

I shake my head.

"Good. Because then I'd have to find your ma and kill her, and I don't know if I could do it exactly the way you'd want it done." Abel's grin widens.

And I have no choice but to smile in response. "You can't handle that quite yet."

He shrugs and leads me to the bed, only settling beside me after he turns off the lamp.

I snuggle into him as a final shiver leaves my body. "I think you're some sort of wizard, Mr. Sommerfeldt," I whisper before kissing his shoulder.

I fall asleep in his arms and dream of blood.

The more that surrounds me, the further Abel becomes until I can't see him anymore.

38 ABEL

BETWEEN MY NIGHTMARES AND THE SIGHT OF ROSE standing at the foot of the bed with a gun to her head, I can't fucking sleep.

I swear I died the moment I saw her and only came back when I realized the click I'd heard was just the goddamn safety.

She sighs in her sleep and I wonder, again, if I'm in over my head. I don't know what I'm doing. Am I helping her? Could I if I really fucking tried or is she just a lost cause?

I pull her in closer as I tell myself *no way*. We have a future together, no matter what it may look like.

No matter what that crock of a doctor said.

The worst part of all this, is that she was at that point because of *me*. I drove her there. It'd be no different if I was the one holding the gun.

I have no idea what I said in my sleep, but I sit until the sun comes up, with the TV on low.

Ma sits in the corner of the room, an empty bottle in her hand, shaking her head at the way my eyes droop just before the fear of sleeping has me jerking awake again.

And, for once, I tell her to fuck right off.

I sit with my Rose all night until morning, guarding over her and protecting her from everything.

Even me.

"I PROMISE EVERYTHING IS PERFECTLY FINE," Rose insists as she starts to take off her clothes and tosses them into the plastic bag she designated as the hamper.

She designated today the day she'll try again to see if her ma is home. This time, I've been invited to go as well.

I nearly miss the sight of her naked ass before she climbs in the shower. She has a scar on her lower back that I never saw before. *Huh?*

"We'll go, and we'll be careful." Her voice is louder over the sound of the shower.

I have to tell myself to keep my ass on the bed and not march into that bathroom, rip the shower curtain open, and pull her onto my eager and waiting dick.

I sigh and sit back on the bed and before I know it, Rose is fully dressed and shaking me awake.

"Will you be okay to drive?" Her eyes are wide and worried as I stretch.

"Yeah, yeah. Let's get this shit over with."

She's wearing all black and I realize she's got on one of my t-shirts. I mention it as she pulls on a denim jacket.

"I love wearing your shirts after you've worn them. It's like wearing a hug."

Rose, for all her smart and emotionless ways, sure can say some cheesy shit.

I pull her into my arms. "I'm not running low or anything," I tell her before I dip down to kiss her.

She pushes away, much to my disappointment. "Come on. I don't want to be out all day."

We get in the car and I'm hoping this goddamn lady is home because it's getting colder and I'm envisioning me and Rose on a beach somewhere far away and warm.

Fuck New England winters.

She's rubbing her hands together as I try to crank the heat as quickly as possible. I love the way she looks with pink cheeks; if it's from embarrassment or the cold, I don't care.

"Think she'll be there today?"

Her eyes meet mine and she sits back with a sigh. "If she isn't, we'll leave."

I can feel her eyes on me as I look back at the parking lot we're pulling out of.

"And somewhere down the line, when they've all but forgotten about us, we'll come back," she says.

Those words, moments like these, make it so easy to fall more and more in love with her. "You're fucking great, you know that?" I turn the steering wheel to take a right onto a street.

"Great? That isn't an adjective I've heard when used to describe me before."

When we're out on the road, she starts messing with the radio, but I'm not done complimenting her.

"You're right. Great is too boring." I tap on the steering wheel as I try to come up with something better. "Awesome?"

She turns in her seat so she's facing me. "I'm not starved for compliments, Mr. Sommerfeldt. Your company is compliment enough."

"I'm shit at words, babe."

"You're better at other things."

"Oh, yeah? Like what?" My eyes are on hers, waiting to see what bullshit she throws my way.

"Saving my life. You're exceptional at that."

I'm a little fucking stunned when she says that. I think about being at Silverwing, when she said she planned to kill herself. I think back to last night and then I wonder what the hell she'd be doing if I wasn't here. Her birthday's coming up, so she'd be getting ready to end it.

The thought makes my grip on the steering wheel tighten so I try to let it go. "I'm just saying I'm not the kind of guy that knows Shakespeare or any of that fancy romantic shit. I might do a little 'roses are red' number or whatever..." I stop when she places her fingers on my cheek. "I'm just not that guy."

"Well let's hear what you come up with then."

Well, fuck.

I glance at her.

Those green eyes. She could ask me for the stars and I'd put them all in a basket for her and watch her light up. I'd deny the world light if she wanted the sun. Screw the rest of the goddamn world.

"Uh...roses are red...violets are blue...some people are dead, but I still love you?"

She picks up my hand and hides her smile behind it. Then she's pressing small kisses to each knuckle. And when she's done she says, "You ain't seen nothin' yet."

And I'm falling in love with her all over again.

39 ROSE

ABEL SINGS ALONG WITH THE RADIO AS WE HEAD toward my old house.

House. Not home.

It feels different this time. I feel as though this is our final stop in this heinous town. I no longer belong here, and Abel never did.

He parks a few houses down from my mother's and I kiss him before I go. Something so normal between two abnormal human beings that have somehow found an emotional connection.

If only Joe could see us now.

Well, not now since I'm creeping up my mother's drive to kill her.

I squat in the bushes for about a half hour when I see a familiar car coming down the bend. Thankfully, Abel's parked far enough away that she shouldn't see him. *If* that's her.

Sure enough, the Mercedes turns into the long driveway and before long, she parks, and the driver's side door opens.

She looks different.

Tired. Older. Bitter.

Her blonde hair has begun to lose its luster and though I'm far enough away, I can see that my once elegant and pristine mother is rather disheveled.

And then it hits me, as I straighten a little to see her clearer.

She's there. She's there and I can't hide my excitement over the idea of *finally* getting vengeance. All these years, I've been patient. And she came home right to me as if she knew I would be here.

She's grabbing her purse and a suitcase from her passenger seat and I'm happy I'm too far to rush and attack her because that's exactly what I'd do. She stands, and I don't know if she can see me when she looks my way, but I stay there anyway.

Part of me wishes I could torment her for a few days. Do things like call and hang up. Tap on her windows when she's home alone. Leave the front door open. These things would drive her to the brink of utter insanity and I'd enjoy every single moment.

But I don't have time for these mind games, no matter how sweet the reward would be. When she walks inside, I rush out of the bushes and run straight toward the car. Abel sees me coming and I can see the question on the tip of his tongue.

Is she there?

"She's here," I tell him as soon as I open the door.

He nods with a look that spells relief. "So, what now?"

I sit back. "Now we wait."

I know exactly how this has to happen and in order for it to be perfect, no one can interrupt us.

I'd been forced to learn early on that no one could be trusted. Certainly not those who insisted on having your trust. Like it was some coveted prize to be won, only for them to destroy it without remorse.

People say trust is like glass. That once it's broken, it can be repaired but the cracks will always be visible.

I wouldn't attempt to repair the glass.

I'd use the shards as weapons against the one who'd broken me.

. . .

IT'S ONE O' clock in the morning. Abel has fallen asleep beside me and I don't blame him. I know he didn't get a lot of sleep last night and we've been sitting here for hours, only leaving to eat and purchase supplies for the task ahead.

One o' clock in the morning and all the houses around us are dark. I reach back to grab the duct tape we bought earlier and open the door, and Abel jolts awake.

"What's going on?" he asks, his voice groggy.

I press my fingers to his lips. "I'll be back. If I take longer than an hour, leave without me."

"Yeah fucking right," he grumbles around my fingers and kisses them.

I drop my hand.

"See you soon, *basherte*."

"Stay here. Don't come inside, no matter what." I don't have to tell him why. I couldn't face causing him more nightmares.

"I'll be right here." He grabs me and kisses me hard.

Before it can go any deeper, I pull away and step out into the cool air. The duct tape is in my hand and I'm ready for anything.

I feel like, for once, the universe is on my side tonight.

My mother hadn't been here before but today...today is special. Like she was being summoned to her death and she'd answered the call.

She had to know what was about to take place.

Just like last time, only quieter, I open the front door with the spare key. I step out of my shoes and leave them by the front door. My footsteps are softer in my socks and I don't want her to hear me coming. The house is dark but maneuvering through my old home is nearly effortless.

I slide one of the kitchen drawers open and I have to squint but there it is—the perfect knife. Careful not to touch any of the others, I grab it and wipe it against the sleeve of my jacket.

Will she know why I chose this specific one?

My steps are steady as I walk up the stairs. Quiet but steady. My grip on the knife handle is tight.

Some people think that you should never kill your parents. I shouldn't kill my mother because she was the vessel that brought me to this life.

She was also the vessel that drove me straight to hell.

So tonight, I see my mother as nothing more than a vehicle. No sentimental value; just like the car Abel is sitting in.

I'm close to her room when I hear the hum of conversation.

She's still awake?

I step closer to the door that's cracked open.

"Why haven't you contacted the police? Why is no one doing anything about this? She could be waiting for me right now, Dr. Brown."

I can't help my smile.

Yes, the universe is my friend tonight.

"Well you don't know Rosamunde as well as I do. She doesn't think the way the rest of us do." She steps toward the window where I can see her peeking out into the night.

Too late, mother. I'm already here to kill you.

"I'll have to contact the police. Please call my cell from now on." She pauses. "No, I know I hadn't provided that information. Because I expected you to be a little better at your job, Dr. Brown, and now *I* have to worry about her. Do you see how this is a little inconvenient?"

She glances at the door and when I see her head toward me, I slink back into the office and push the door so it's only enough for me to look out of.

She swings her door open and looks out into the hall. "Yes. Yes, I understand. I'll wait. Fine. Have a good night, Dr. Brown." She doesn't wait for his response, just hangs up and mutters the words "incompetent fool" to herself in soliloquy.

I almost forgot how rude my mother was.

I step out of the office just as she sets the phone back down. When she heads toward me, I hide in the office again and listen as she pads down the stairs toward the kitchen.

I hide in the shadows as I watch her pour a glass of red wine and I wonder where Grace has been all this time.

She sets the glass down and walks past where I'm hiding in the doorway, toward the front door.

I rush after her and just as she's about to set the alarm, I grab the back of her hair. "Now, now, Mother. No need to do that." Just as she's about to scream, I press the knife into her neck, just against the vein that I'm sure is pumping with blood. "I don't want to have to slit your throat. I have plans for you. But if you scream, I will."

She gulps, and the tip of the blade digs into her skin, blood beading against it.

"Let's go back upstairs. I'll bet you have a nice fire going in your bedroom."

She nods, and I lead so I'm pulling her by her hair up the stairs.

"Rose, honey..."

"I'm not too keen on being lied to, Mother. I'm not too keen on being lied about. And I'm not too keen on being *stabbed*." I yank her too hard and she stumbles on the stairs. "Up! Get up!"

She cries, and it only serves to annoy me as I start to drag her to her bedroom.

"Oh, Mother, quit," I say as I roll my eyes, pulling her by her hair with one hard tug once we've crossed the threshold into her bedroom. "You had to know this was going to happen."

"I'm sorry."

"Apologies mean nothing when death is at your door. Don't let your end make a liar out of you." I direct her to sit on her bed with my knife. "Touch that phone and it'll be the last thing you do."

I look through her drawers until I find a pair of stockings. I direct her again with the knife, this time to sit on the floor. I tie her hands to her bedpost.

She looks flushed as the flames in the fireplace flicker over the room.

"Comfortable?" I ask, and she shivers as she nods. "Still lying, I see." That she'd bother to lie to me now is quite comical. "I'm wondering what you're sorry for, Mother." The knife is heavy in my hand. *Kill, kill, kill,* it says but I'm in charge. For once, I'm in charge.

"For all of it. For lying and putting you in that place." She says the words like they taste bitter.

It's beautiful, what human beings will do for survival. For my mother, she'll face her terrible decisions with regret.

Regret.

Perhaps her lack of regret was passed onto me.

It was her brokenness that mine was born of. The only difference is, she will face regret.

I wonder what it will feel like.

My eyes wander the room and land on her closet. I give her one final glance, pinning her with a glare, before heading to her closet.

I know what I'm looking for before I even catch sight of it.

There, in the back of the closet, hanging innocently, looking far plainer than it actually is, is the black dress I used to try on time and again, wondering when I'd be woman enough to fill the slinky material.

I strip out of my clothes quickly, kicking them into a pile before yanking the dress from its hanger and sliding it over my skin.

I run my hands down my hips to smooth and bunching material as I take a look at myself.

Black. Backless.

Dangerous.

Finally, woman enough.

I tiptoe back into the bedroom and smirk at my mother. "I used to want to look as perfectly as you did in this dress. Now the idea of it sickens me."

Me, with my hair undone, my face plain, and my eyes wild.

Her, with her hair soft and silken, her makeup running down her face, and her eyes pleading.

Grace always looked more like her than I did.

"Where's Grace?" I want to know she won't be the one to find my mother.

My mother's eyes fill all over again. "You haven't heard."

I press the knife flat against her chin. "What is it?"

"Grace is gone. She committed suicide a few months ago. I found her…"

I'm momentarily stopped. The world stops. I stop breathing. And then I start again. "Liar," I whisper, the blade catching the light as it shakes in my unsteady grip.

She winces when the tip punctures her skin. "Why would I lie about that? What do I gain?"

Her words are frantic, but I can't understand why. "How? Why?"

My mother is looking at me like I'm insane. *Who asks how someone took their life*, she must be wondering.

Me, mother. Always me.

"She hung herself. Her note blamed me. You. Her father. Some boy named George."

George?

There's only one George I can think of and I don't know what that snide little moron has to do with Grace.

I don't want my mother to see me cry. She doesn't deserve to see anything other than the monster she created. "Where's the note?"

She points to the office. She's probably thinking this will buy her time. And she's right.

I have to see Grace's suicide letter for myself. I grab the duct tape from the pile in the closet, rip off a strip and place it over her mouth. "I'll be back. I suggest while I'm gone, you behave yourself. What's meant to be relatively quick can easily be drawn out."

Her eyes are wide as I turn away and head toward my father's office. I use the tip of the knife, dragging it against the wall and up to turn on the light. I could nearly see him sitting there, and when I walk in, he would look up at me with a smile.

But that time is gone, and I remind myself of that as I open the top drawer. I recognize Grace's handwriting immediately.

She doesn't address anyone in the note, getting right to her message.

I PROBABLY WON'T BE FOUND for a few days. My mother has gone on another one of her vacations. At least I have the satisfaction of knowing she'll be the one to find me.

My father wasn't a bad person. He didn't deserve to die.

But my sister wasn't a bad person, either.

I can't say the same for my mother.

I can't say the same for the man that…

I STOP READING and fold the letter up before pulling the bottom of the dress up and shoving the letter into the side of my panties.

This letter is sucking the violence from my body and I can't.

If I keep reading, I'll be lost in my emotions. I run my fingers over the blade that is still in my hand.

George will have to die. He is now as etched on my list as the scar in my back.

And so, I square my shoulders and walk back into my mother's room. She's struggling against her tied stockings and I fight the urge to snicker. She'd tell me it was unladylike, and I'd tell her that stabbing my mother in the neck might be even worse.

"I'm guessing you didn't know?" I ask, and she turns to look at me, her face pink from exertion. She shakes her head and I shake mine too. "Of course, you didn't."

She cries against the tape like I should care about her feelings. Not when she's ruined so many lives.

"At least you'll die knowing both your daughters were avenged," I mutter.

All while she sits there, I look around, remembering a time when my father influenced this room. All traces of him are gone now. How sad it is that even in the home *he* built, he's gone. Only one room remains the same and it's less a memorial than it is a badge of cowardice.

The knife in my hand speaks to me. It has tasted my blood, it knows my language. It understands me well.

Kill her, it screams.

I want to shout back but the time has come.

I turn to look at her and smile. She starts to cry but the sound of her fear falls on deaf ears.

I'm not so far gone that I don't realize that most people don't go around killing other people. I know this isn't the *norm*. But if the world taught me anything, it was to treat others accordingly.

Perhaps it was the universe's fault. Maybe it was mine. These minor details don't matter anymore.

Not when I'm brandishing my knife and taking another step toward my mother. It's strange that the knife that's about to kill her is the same knife she slid into my flesh the moment my father was dead.

Maybe I am a murderer.

Perhaps I am insane.

But the moment I turned in shock, blood already sliding down my back, I saw the momentary glee in her eyes. My violence came from this woman. You can't compete with that high and someone using the same drug will always recognize the ephemeral euphoria. I recognize the monster I am, deep in her eyes, hidden behind the golden irises that are now filling with tears.

"Remember this knife, Mother? It's the same knife you stabbed me in the back with after I killed your husband." A smile curves before I can stop it. "Surely you can find the poetic justice in this. The hilarity, I'd even dare to say."

I sink to my knees in front of her and her eyes are pleading with me but I neither care for them nor the words she might say, given the chance.

I press my ear against her chest and I can hear the unsteady thud of her heartbeat. It moves so quickly against her that I wish I could hold it in my hand and watch it still, no longer having to be attached to such a venomous human being.

"I want to carve your heart out of your chest, Mother. Just to see if it exists." I lean back, away from her, ignoring her tears. "But that isn't part of the plan."

She cries against the tape over her mouth, but I can't hear her. I can't hear her beg. I can't hear her lies. I can only hear the truth, the words she whispered to me years ago before I stepped out of my room to help her. Those whispered words of deception created the perfect bridge to help me cross over to my doom. She was the gatekeeper of my own personal hell and I wouldn't let her do this to anyone else.

I grab one of her wrists and cut the pantyhose away from her skin before pressing my lips to her pulse.

Without a word, the silver glint of the blade shines as I slide it against her wrist. The blood, deeply maroon and already pouring from her wound, makes me dizzy with delight. I quickly slice her other wrist and stand. I catch my reflection in the mirror above the fireplace and I admire the sparkle in my eye.

In my madness, I am beautiful.

I glance down at my mother and she's pressing her bloody wrists to her chest.

She would ruin her silk blouse?

My mind goes over the way I pictured this going in my head.

Oh, yes. *Let her scream.*

I rip the duct tape from her lips and step back again as she screams. She pauses to inhale and scream again but this time, I join her.

Her voice cracks and she looks at me with a small shake of her head.

"You're a monster, Mother. And that's exactly what you've made of me."

If every second is a series of dominoes, my mother's actions are the force behind the knife I'm about to shove in her esophagus. I glance down at it, admiring the blood that's already stained the sleek metal. What a beautiful domino.

"Rose, honey. You don't have to do this."

"No. I don't have to."

She inhales and exhales, a small smile flitting over her lips for a moment.

"I want to." I grab the golden strands at her crown. All of this gold. "And certainly before Abel gets worried."

Now. Now. Now!

There's a small part of me that wants to press the blade into her skin slowly but that *isn't* the plan, either. I have to do things exactly the way I pictured. I have to.

One, two, three, four...

I jerk my hand back and then shove it forward, into the flesh of her neck, licking my lips when I feel the warmth of her blood hitting my hand and smattering my face with color.

This shade is crimson and it's the crimson I've been craving since entering this terrible place.

40 ABEL

THE RADIO IS ON LOW AND THE SOUND OF IT KEEPS ME
company as we head back to the motel. My eyes droop from time
to time, in the silence between the two of us, but I manage to get
us back without crashing.

She hasn't touched me since she left that house, like she left a
piece of herself inside. The part that makes her *alive*. And I want
nothing more than to reach out and break whatever trance she's in.

But I don't know what's going on in her head, so I let her stay
inside it, working out whatever the hell she needs to, hoping her
mind—her twisted fucking violence—will give her back to me at
some point.

41 ROSE

I'M COLD IN THIS DRESS, MY HARD NIPPLES PRESSED against the black fabric in protest of the breeze that hits my body as soon as I open the bathroom window.

Abel is on the other side of the door, likely wondering why I've locked myself in this tiny space.

It hugs me. Much like the room at Silverwing, only without its bleach and urine scents. I don't count. There is no fear.

I don't quite know what there is, but I revel in the familiarity of this moment.

There, in the corner, my jacket sits. My hands are still wearing my mother's blood as I reach for it—the knife in the pocket. I don't react when the blade pokes my finger. Once it's in my grip, I head toward the sink and toss it down.

I don't want to touch the letter—the only thing my sister left behind—with these filthy hands. But the words will not stop circling around in my head, making me feel faint with such foreign and piercing emotions.

She's gone.

When I lift my head, my reflection shocks me, with its glassy eyes and sorrowful expression.

I yearn to cut it from my body. To be as cold as I've been all along.

But I can't. I glance at the door. A reminder that the person on the other side of it has brought too much warmth to my world.

And so, the internal struggle of being who he deserves and fighting who I am waxes and wanes on as I reach for the knife again.

42 ABEL

I'M LYING IN BED, WITH THE LIGHT OFF, WHEN ROSE finally decides to open the bathroom door. The light is off in there, too, so I'm faced with a creepy shadow of the woman I love.

Real fucking fitting.

"I can't see you," I whisper, and she stops in front of me. *Why the fuck am I whispering?*

She reaches over and flicks the switch to the lamp on the nightstand and the moment I see her eyes, I wonder if she's gonna kill me, too. They're too direct, too confident, too fucking intense. But they're glassy, like she's on the edge of some emotion I don't understand.

And then I notice her hair.

It's gone.

Well, not *all* gone. But it sits in a mess of locks at her shoulders. Some of it is tinged with red and I want to pull her close, to make sure she isn't hurt or bleeding.

But those fucking eyes stop me.

I stand. But that's all I have the nerve to do.

My eyes follow the lines of her body in this dress that does nothing to hide every detail. From her nipples, to the dip of her belly button, even to the space between her thighs that I'm dying to fill. I lick my lips as I look back at her.

I'm a statue as she tilts her chin and parts her perfect lips. She steps closer to me, so close that I can feel her breath on my neck.

There's something in her eyes that makes me think, *this is it*. This is the moment I've been waiting for ever since my eyes dropped to those pink fucking lips.

Her hand grips the back of my neck and pulls me toward her but that's all I'm about to let her do to me. I grab her even closer, my palms on her ass, squeezing and bracing. Words would feel cheap and corny right now. All I want is her body and the way she's moving against me tells me she wants mine, too.

She bites my lip and tucks those small hands in my shirt but I'm no fucking fool. Not today, anyway. I know what those things are capable of. The long marks in my skin are proof of her need to inflict pain, even when she's feeling pleasure.

I press her back against the nearest wall and pin her with my hips before grabbing her wrists and holding them above her head. She wriggles and tries to fight but I kiss her before she can over-think and overanalyze. She said she's never experienced an orgasm and in order for me to change that, I have to strip her of her identity.

We have to be two people who really want to fuck.

Not two people in love with the monsters inside of each other.

I grab the ends of her dress and yank it up, pulling the backs of her legs so they wrap around my body.

When she rolls her hips, I feel a groan rumble in the back of my throat. I cup her face and she pulls my hair before biting my neck. It hurts so much that I drop her and turn her to face the wall. I'm rough, each touch causing her to push the air from her body like she's surprised.

Yeah. I'm not like those other motherfuckers.

Her bare back is to me and it's obvious she's naked underneath. I push my erection into the soft flesh of her ass and press a kiss between her shoulder blades. She sounds breathless as I yank at the top of her dress, pulling the straps away and letting it slide down. It's halfway off, stopped at her hips, when I press her chest into the wall and slap her ass.

Her gasp makes it easier to continue. I'm not worried about Rose. I don't give a fuck about what she thinks she knows about sex or anything else in the world.

I'm gonna take everything she thought she knew and prove her wrong. With every lick, stroke, and fuck, I'm gonna make her see that the high killing gives her is nothing compared to this.

Her body moves with each inhale and exhale and I push the rest of the dress down until she's naked in front of me. My fingers brush her scar and she stiffens for a moment. But I waste no time sliding my hand toward her pussy and after a few rubs, I smack it, making her cry out and spread her legs a little farther apart.

She probably doesn't even realize that her body is opening up for me. I lick the space between her neck and shoulder before biting down, my hand back to rubbing her swollen lips. I can't stop there. No stopping when she leans forward and sticks her ass out a little. One finger enters her slowly and my other hand plays with her clit.

Maybe someone like me doesn't know shit about shit. But I guarantee I can make Rose come.

At this point, I'm completely avoiding my own needs, my dick attempting to pitch a tent in my jeans. Her ass brushes against it and I pause. She's breathing like she's just finished running for her life. Or maybe toward an orgasm. But I can't think as I press two fingers into her this time, still rubbing and pinching her clit.

I can tell it's coming. I fucking know it more than I know my own goddamn name. Her breaths are shortening. Her eyes are unfocused as she presses her cheek against the wall and even under the dim lighting, I can see her skin getting pinker and pinker.

And then I hear one high-pitched gasp followed by another.

"Don't stop," she whispers, her words nearly lost in those gasps that make my dick even harder.

As if I fucking would.

She's damn near riding my hand *hard*. As she slows, I grab her hair and press my lips against her ear. "I can't wait to see what you look like with my dick inside you." I yank her hair so her chin lifts as she sags against the wall. "But not tonight."

No way would the night she killed her ma be the first time we have sex.

I press one last kiss to her neck and walk away, leaving her breathless and holding onto the wall for dear life.

I need a fucking shower and probably the rest of the night with my dick in my hands.

Fuck.

BY THE TIME I get out of the shower, having jerked my shit until it was damn near raw, Rose is sleeping in the bed, her dress a pile of forgotten fabric on the floor.

That's what a good orgasm'll do to you: put your ass right to sleep.

I sit down beside her, and she wiggles a little in her sleep, a frown creasing the skin between her eyebrows. I reach over and rub my thumb over her cheek. I can only fucking *imagine* what today was like.

She wiggles again before turning over and when she settles, I see the silvery scar where the blanket isn't covering her. Whatever broke through her skin left a clean scar, straight and to the point, unlike the ones I wear.

The crooked L on my back. Half a fucking swastika courtesy of my ma. The ones on my knees from being pushed around by bullies and the man I called my dad for so long. The ones on my elbows from making sure I didn't break my fucking face when I fell.

I reach down and kiss the scar Rose hasn't told me about because whatever the fuck it was that happened to her, it'd caused her pain.

And I didn't want that shit for her anymore.

43 ROSE

A WOMAN YELLS OUTSIDE OUR ROOM AND I OPEN MY
eyes, waiting to feel if Abel is awake. So far, the room is silent and
still. And then he lets out a deep sigh, even and quiet.

Those fingers that'd been inside me were curled up just beside
his face. Those fingers that'd given me the most pleasurable experience of my life.

The man who'd spanked me *unlike* I was a child, making my
body clench with elation. But it was worse than liking it; it was this
idea that I'd deserved the sting of pain accompanied by the dip of
pleasure.

I'd never known anything in my entire existence that could
make me as disoriented, as divided, as Abel when his hand
smacked my bottom. Now that it's happened, it's all I can think
about. I even allow myself to wonder when it'll happen again.

This time a man starts yelling and I have to clench my fists, so I
don't get up and shoot them both. As if they know what I want to
do, I hear a car door shutting, an engine starting, and someone
pulling away. All is quiet again as I roll over onto my back.

I stare at the ceiling, and the sounds of each of Abel's exhales remind me that the world is without one person this morning. I imagine, or hope, it'll take the authorities a little while to find her dead body in that empty house that no one visits.

I am the last of the Montgomerys.

Abel is the last of the Sommerfeldts.

We are the ones that will last.

In my hope, I am buoyant. Foolishly so.

As I mull over these thoughts, Abel's breathing begins to shorten, and he turns to face me before opening his eyes slowly.

I should be blinded by the bright blue irises. That his mother had hated him because of them makes me itch to desecrate her grave.

"Show me your pain," I whisper, like it's a secret only he and I can know.

Abel reaches for my hand. His is much warmer than mine and I squeeze his for a moment before he slides his palm down so he's holding onto my fingers and pressing them to the skin on the back of his shoulder. I can feel it, raised and bumpy under my fingers but I want to see it, so I sit up.

It looks like he has an upside-down L in his skin, deep down where his little bit of pigment is stored. It looks innocent enough except I'd heard the story and I know that scar wasn't an accident. There'd be no funny anecdote to follow.

I can only offer my sad silence as I run my fingers over it again and again. He doesn't move, only the slight rise of his form as he inhales, then lowering again as he exhales.

I wonder if Abel screamed as she did it. I wonder how much he bled. And I think about the type of weapon she used. Whatever it was, it had to have been dull. It had to have required running over and over his skin in order to break it because the scar is uneven and jagged. I didn't ask Abel these things because I secretly worry that the more intense and personal my questions become, the more he'll see through the image I've tried to hold in place.

Love can heal, people say. *Love can change you,* I've heard.

Love can do all these things, but it'll never make me stop killing people. I still crave it. Only now, afterwards, I come home to Abel and let him love me.

That's love, in my world: saving the best parts of yourself for that one person and giving your worst to the rest of the world.

Like the woman who carved the scar into Abel's skin.

If I could bring Abel's mother back, I would. So I could slit her throat and call it even. But I know such things aren't in my power. Just as I know I wouldn't be able to simply slit her throat. I'd cause pain, enough that her screams would make *my* toes curl.

Abel turns over on his back and sits up. "What's goin' on in that head of yours?" he asks.

And I don't want to lose the way he looks at me so I lie. "Nothing." *Just thinking of all the ways I'd kill your mother if I could.*

It's the first time I've ever lied to Abel. But if I lie with good intentions, surely it can't be as bad as others make it out to be. I'm lying to save us. To save him from watching the person he loves turn into someone he doesn't recognize.

He may think he's already seen me at my worst, but he hasn't.

I can get even messier.

"Show me yours?" he asks. He doesn't whisper the way I did.

And I wonder if it's because my pain isn't our secret. My pain is merely the beginning of everyone else's.

I lift myself higher and pause. Abel's eyes are on my breasts. They're not very big but I like the way he stills and stares. I look down and learn that my nipples like it, too.

I try to turn over, but Abel does it for me, pulling me back and turning me in one fluid motion until I'm sitting up and my back is facing him. I can feel how warm he is, and I hunch forward a little so he can see where my mother shoved the blade inside me.

"What happened?" he asks.

"Everything is slightly fuzzy before it happened, like a dream. I was so invested in what I was doing, hitting him over and over, almost like I was asleep. And then he wasn't moving anymore and I kind of woke up. I saw my mother standing behind me with a kitchen knife in her hand. Before I could ask her what she was doing, she stabbed me. She stabbed me, so she could make it seem like I was alone in the act. Like I was going to kill her next." I exhale, remembering the sound of her frantic lies when she called the police. I was bleeding so much, I'm surprised I was conscious. "I felt like a fool."

Abel starts to knead my shoulders and I groan, my head tilting back.

"She can't hurt you anymore, *basherte.*" He whispers those words against my skin like my revenge should only stay between us.

And it should. If anyone found out, they'd take me away again. I'd fill graves before that happened.

"What shall we do today, Mr. Sommerfeldt?" I ask as I turn to face him, changing the subject. I bring my legs up toward my chest and hug them.

He smiles and presses a kiss to one of my knees. "If I told you what *I* wanted to do, you'd be scared of me."

I open my mouth to argue but he kisses my lips.

"Someone's birthday is tomorrow," he says. "Let's throw you a fucking party."

I can't help the cock of my eyebrow at the sound of a party. "You do realize we'd have to have *friends* to achieve the type of party I'm sure you're used to."

He rolls over with a groan, shoving his face into a pillow. "People are lame any fucking way." He peeks up at me, one eye looking at me, the other covered by his arm.

I press my lips together to keep from smiling. "Did you have friends before?"

Before, before.

He blinks one eye and I wonder if I have to explain what I mean when I say "before".

Before Rose.

Before Silverwing.

Before being my salvation.

"I thought I did even before everything happened. I had friends in high school but then Ma died, and I had nowhere to go. Graduated high school and everyone kinda disappeared. It wasn't always fun, being me."

I place my hand on his head and run my fingers lightly over his hair, which is silky and sliding against my fingertips. I envy his hair. I would love nothing more than to live against him, to be perpetually warmed by him. To die with him. To live with him his whole life.

"By the time I got arrested, I was just trying to stay alive."

I stop stroking his hair.

What would the world be like without Abel?

The thought alone makes me shiver. "A lot of people would sympathize with you. Some would even empathize," I say, not offering either.

"And you?"

That one eye staring up at me may have seen my lips twitch at the idea of sweet satisfaction. "I'd like to hurt every person that ever hurt you. I'm not sure if anyone in the world understands that but you."

He's quiet and I worry.

In my worry, I am the clouds rolling in and he is the wind that pushes me.

His eyes show me nothing, his mouth unmoving and hidden from me.

"I do," he whispers.

He says those two words like a vow, like they're binding.

"I love you, you know," I tell him as I slide down and reach for his arm, placing it over me so I can move against him and kiss his nose.

He shifts to face me and I can see all of his face.

"I know," he says.

Love can change you. Love can heal you.

Love can stop the storm from rolling in and destroying the world around you.

44 ABEL

WE DRIVE FAR OUT OF TOWN TODAY, ALMOST THREE hours from the motel. We're somewhere in Connecticut when I see a sign for a mall and take the exit.

Thank fuck.

"You feel like shopping?" Rose asks.

I didn't know if she was awake or not, she'd been so quiet.

"I feel like seeing you in something nice. Something new." I hadn't told her the plan for today. I just needed to get us the fuck out of the state of New York and out of that damn motel room. I wanted to remind Rose that she was fucking *free*. We could do whatever the hell we wanted. We didn't have to stay in that godforsaken town now that her ma was dead.

All this mishegas, mine would say, sitting in the backseat with a lit cigarette between her dry, stubby fingers.

I fight the urge to check the backseat, just to see if the heat on my neck is from her disapproving glare. I roll my eyes at the thought before looking over at Rose, whose eyes are taking in our surroundings now that we're around something other than trees.

I want to open my mouth and tell this girl what I'm thinking but there's the nagging feeling that I have no right to tell her what to do. After all, we're fucking wanted. At least, we should be, but we watch the news every day, and every day we hear jack shit.

We're still pressing our luck.

We should be fucking running.

But something is telling me something's off about this. She hasn't made a move to leave. I know it's only the day after, but we haven't talked about what's next. Rose is smarter than I am, but I know more about surviving. And staying here is just fucking dumb. We're gonna get caught.

I park the car far away from the others and turn it off. When I turn to face Rose, she's already facing me, and her jacket is open enough that I can see the outline of her nipples against her shirt.

It's like she doesn't believe in bras. Or maybe she just wants to drive me out of my fucking brain.

I reach up, slowly, slow enough that she can stop me if she wants.

But she doesn't.

Not when I circle the outside of her soft nipple, watching as it hardens for me, because of me.

Not when I cradle her small breast in my palm. Not even when I run my thumb over the hardened peak, the side of my lips lifting at the way hers part and her hips buck a little in her seat.

"I never knew it could feel like this," she whispers.

"Like what, *sheyn royz?*"

She nearly purrs, "Like my body's on fire and you lit the match."

Her hands reach out to grab my arms and I draw her closer, one hand still stroking her nipple, the other on her jaw.

Tongues tasting, teeth scraping, bodies aching for more.

I jump away from her when I feel her hand on my dick.

Her eyes are closed for a moment and I want to remember what she looks like right now. I want to remember the power I have over her, that she could forget herself and follow what her body wants. That she could do something so fucking *bold* and unapologetic.

"Do you not want me?" she asks as she leans back, her head against the glass of the passenger window.

And I have a newfound weakness: sunlight and green eyes. The way hers sparkle with curiosity makes me want to place her hand back on my dick so she knows without a doubt that I want her.

My hand reaches for hers without thought, and instead, I press kisses to her fingertips. "You know better than that, Rose."

"Why did we stop?" She leans forward and her breasts sway ever so slightly with the movement.

"Because you deserve better than a quickie in the car." I reach for the door but pause and smirk before opening it. "For our first time, anyway."

She follows me out and I wonder if it's a good idea for us to be out in public. I wonder if anyone will recognize us. I wonder if Rose can handle people. And I wonder if today will be the day that our faces are plastered on every television screen.

I even wonder how much longer we can live a life like this, all fucked and feeling followed. The moment I decided to take responsibility for Rose's life, my dreams burned to the goddamn ground.

But when her hand reaches for mine, I take it without hesitation.

Because I've never had someone so invested in me. I've never had someone look at me the way she does, like the world won't continue without me in it.

"It's your fault," she tells me as we head for the mall entrance.

"What is?"

"The inappropriate touching."

I grin as I look at her, but she doesn't give me the satisfaction of her stare.

"You created a monster," she says.

I want to tell her that the monsters in both of us had nothing to do with the other, but I choose to be light-hearted instead. "Nothing was inappropriate about what you did." I pull her in front of me as I grab the door and guide her inside. "Besides, I'm the only monster around when you're naked, Rose."

I don't see her reaction, and while we walk, she's quiet. People don't pay us any attention, and I keep her close, hoping she doesn't get set off by anything.

"Would you like to see a movie?" I ask after we've passed by an entire floor of stores, none of them catching Rose's interest.

She nods, her eyes everywhere but on me.

"Let's see what's playing," I say. I relax a little as we head to the top floor, knowing that at least while we're seated in the theater, I won't have to worry about what trouble we could get into.

Rose doesn't care what movie we see as she leaves me to head to the concession stand. I'm so focused on her, that I don't realize I'm holding the line up until someone behind me clears her throat.

"Sorry about that," I mutter, and I turn for a moment to offer a quick smile to the person behind me.

She's standing next to another girl and her long brown hair is shining even under the dim lights of the theater lobby.

"No problem."

After I have two tickets to some random movie that starts in the next ten minutes, I hear her speak again.

"A rare breed, seeing a chick flick on your own. Takes a certain kind of man."

Her friend walks up, past me, no doubt to buy tickets, too. But the brunette stands where she is to talk to me.

Another small smile and I hold up my two tickets. "Nah, I'm here with my girlfriend."

"Lucky her," she says, her smile slow and lingering, and finally follows her friend.

When I turn to find Rose, she's standing a few feet away, popcorn and a drink in her hands. Her eyes flicker back and forth between me and the brunette.

She doesn't look angry. She doesn't look like she's going to lash out.

But I'm still cautious as I approach. "Got our tickets, *basherte*."

She's quiet as we head into the theater. A few minutes later, I hear voices, just as the lights start to dim. The girl from the lobby sits a few rows away from of us, and they laugh about something.

I try to read Rose's body language, but she's sitting next to me, gathering a few pieces of popcorn before daintily placing them in her mouth.

Not like me, stuffing as many as I can into this fucking face of mine.

She shoots me a glance as I'm chewing, and there's a hint of a smile on her face.

And I think that Dr. Brown would be so fucking proud of us.

The movie begins just as she relaxes into my arms.

45 ROSE

I TRY TO FOCUS ON THE MOVIE.

I give a sincere effort.

But the girl seated a few rows from me and Abel is going to die.

I never thought something as trivial as jealousy would plague me. But this feels much more suffocating than something as simple as that.

It feels like a direct threat to my lifeblood.

So, when she stands—to use the restroom, no doubt—I whisper that I'm going as well. Abel is so engrossed in the film, his hand full of buttery popcorn, that he only offers a nod.

The restroom is quiet as I walk in and step quietly toward the stalls. I notice her black ballet flats peeking from beneath the door.

So as not to alarm the other patron, I get in the stall across from her. There's this giddy part of me that wants to kick her door in and take it from there. To let my violence take over, with no plan, with nothing but her pain as my destination. I hear the toilet flush as the adrenaline spikes in me, making my hands shake. Her stall door opens, and she slips out. I push mine open just enough to see her stare at her reflection for a few moments before reaching for the soap dispenser.

I'm quiet as I push my door open the rest of the way. Because I assume this relatively sentient human being will become aware of my presence and will see me. And once she does, I have to move quickly.

Or not.

Maybe I'll play a little this time.

Her eyes are on her hands as she rubs them together beneath the water. Her gaze flickers to me for a moment. And then down and up again. She's recognized me.

But from where? I can almost *hear* her ask herself that question.

I'm the girl from the lobby. The one you glanced at just before you tried to take Abel from me.

"You look so familiar," I tell her, my voice sounding an octave higher than usual. "What's your name?"

"Mackenzie," she offers, hesitantly. "Yours?"

She's only asked out of an ingrained politeness. She doesn't know it's wasted on me.

~~Selene Montgomery~~
  George
  Mackenzie

MY LIST GROWS.

She doesn't recognize me.

Until I drop the hint. "That's right. You were the one who hit on my boyfriend."

And I can see the moment it all connects in her brain. Her mouth opens and her eyes widen.

There's probably an apology or some claim of misunderstanding on the tip of her tongue, but no.

A scream should be forcing its way up instead.

But she has no idea.

How could she know that she'd meet me today? That I would become the most powerful person in her existence?

She should scream.

Biologically, we know when our lives are threatened. Our body has something we've come to call "instinct" and it's a powerful thing. But we've been so conditioned, so softened by our desires, that we forget to listen to our instincts.

Your instincts will save you.

By now, it's too late to call for help. I've already gripped the back of her neck and forced her face into the mirror several times until she slid lifelessly to the floor.

Some deaths are drawn out and painful.

Mackenzie got lucky.

There's no blood on my skin, none under my fingernails, but I still wash my hands thoroughly. I stare at the lifeless body behind me in the mirror, past my own reflection, not quite smiling, but not frowning either.

Just as the blood oozes slowly from her skull, thick and dark, I step over her and head back toward Abel.

He's exactly where I left him when I return, smiling around a mouthful of popcorn when he sees me. He offers me some and smiles wider when I place a few pieces in my mouth.

And I want him to look at me like this forever.

46 ABEL

I ROLL MY EYES AS THE CREDITS START ROLLING AND turn to Rose.

"I hope this movie didn't give you any ideas."

"What do you mean?" she asks as we head toward the exit.

"I don't think anyone is ever as romantic as they portray in these movies."

"You've already proven to be quite the poet, Mr. Sommerfeldt," she says as her hand slides into mine.

I notice we're the only ones in the theater, everyone else apparently having gone while we slowly made our way out.

It's just the two of us as I stop her with my free hand on her abdomen. She halts, like I'm that in control.

Fuck, I love touching her. I love how this relationship is so dominated by her but with everything physical, it's like she's my puppet.

She's staring with wide eyes as I slide my hand down toward her jeans, pulling at the waist and popping the top button open.

I'm still holding her hand, and I bring it up to kiss it as I pull her zipper down, just enough to slip my free hand inside.

There's this little inhale, so fucking quiet that if I hadn't been staring at her, I would've missed it.

We're standing in the middle of the aisle with my fingers stroking her, fingers getting wetter by the fucking moment.

"Tell me what you want," I whisper against her lips.

Before she has a moment to answer, there's a loud thud outside the door and we're jumping apart.

"Come on," I tell her.

The closer we get to the exit, the more I hear people shuffling, and then a loud cry.

I pull Rose close. Whatever's beyond this door, I need to protect her. I stick my head out first and see a group of workers surrounding the girls' bathroom. And then the girl from before, the one that'd been with the brunette...

She's sobbing, blood on her hands.

"Rose," I whisper. I can't look at her. I can't face her as I let the door shut, closing us back in the empty theater.

The monster and me.

What did you do?

"What the fuck did you do?" When I do face her, it's like I don't even recognize the person in front of me. "Who *are* you?"

And what the fuck are you capable of?

"The same person whose pants you just had your hand down."

It's all so fucked.

The horniness has given way to terror.

It's so fucking twisted.

What the hell is my life now?

I want to ask her why but I'm fucking terrified of her answer. I'm terrified that it'll be something impossible to get over.

But who the fuck am I kidding? This entire thing is impossible to get over.

She reaches for my face when I try to break eye contact. So much pressure, so many emotions, all of them connected to this one person who is both the highest goddamn high and the lowest of the lows.

"It's like I don't even know you," I say when her focus just bounces between both my eyes, like she's trying to read everything I don't even know how the hell to express. "You're my Rose. And then you're something else entirely."

A motherfucking nightmare.

"I'll never hurt you, Abel, but I'll kill to keep you. Even if that means killing every other woman you might attempt to find happiness with. You may think this is crazy, but you believe the same thing in so many words. That we're meant to be. That I'm your *basherte.* You make destiny sound so lovely. All I'm doing is cementing your destiny."

Her grip on my face tightens for a second before she lets go and steps back.

"Perhaps I am split in two. Half of me wants to be everything you dream of and half of me can never let go of who I am. But I know that all of me loves you, Abel. That is something that's forever. That's your *basherte.*"

Plag nishmasa, my ma whispers from one of the seats, her lit cigarette making me itch to take a drag.

Old habits I thought I'd gotten rid of itch at the back of my throat.

Plag nishmasa. Half souls.

The stupid as shit idea that we are all half souls, walking around the earth, waiting for our other half.

But, instead of waiting for her second half, instead of waiting for me, Rose filled it with violence.

And it would always be her first love.

I can't think as I grab her arm and we head out the door. People are either running around or standing still, wondering what's going on. I make eye contact with the girl who's still sobbing. She looks past me, at the person just beside me, and I instinctively hide my monster behind me.

We walk out of the theater, but not before I look up at one of the many cameras hidden under a bubble-like covering in the ceiling.

The eyes in the sky.

They'll see us, and they'll post our images for everyone to see.

They'll call her a murderer and they'll say I helped.

And maybe I'm innocent of this act, but every one of her actions is my fault.

We make it outside and I take a deep breath, my eyes wide and watching.

Dead leaves are on the ground. We're surrounded by dead things. This is our fucking life now.

47 ROSE

EIGHT-HUNDRED AND SIXTY-TWO, EIGHT HUNDRED AND SIXTY-THREE...

Abel is silent. There's no music, nothing but the hum of the engine as we speed back toward where we came from.

And so, in an effort to keep from tumbling into my mind, I count.

But there is no stopping the inevitable. There is no delaying destiny. And I think of Grace, in spite of myself. I think of my little sister, who was the only good thing in my life.

Everything my parents had hoped for in me, they had found in her. It was no wonder they had another child after me. Like they knew I was going to be this vampire of a girl, craving blood in a way that sustained my life, albeit mentally more than physically. Or perhaps emotionally.

Regardless, there she'd been—all smiles and laughter. And I loved her enough to assume that I'd bear the weight of the bad, so she could be the good one.

And I accepted that.

We never fought. We never angered each other, yet I wasn't foolish enough to think I managed to live all this time with her without disappointing her.

If I'd mistakenly thought so, her suicide note proved otherwise.
But George...

Abel coughs and my focus snaps back to the present.

I'd have to explain to Abel. I'd have to get him to see that we couldn't leave just yet.

48 ABEL

WE'VE JUST WALKED INSIDE THE MOTEL ROOM WHEN I reach for her wrist and pull her back to me. There's something in her eyes when I look at her.

They study my face and they flinch.

Fear.

I'm delivering it and she's giving it right fucking back.

And I ask the question I've been wanting to ask since I realized what the fuck she's truly capable of. "Will I ever be enough for you?"

Silence.

Her mouth opens and closes. And then she's grabbing me and pulling me to her.

Her kiss feels angry, but I know better. She wants to feel control. But she won't get any of that shit from me when it comes to this. When we touch, I'm in charge.

Her jeans are tight, making it hard to yank them off, but I succeed after sitting on the bed and slowly pulling them down her smooth legs.

Her pussy peeks at me from under her panties and I press my face against it, inhaling the musky scent before running my teeth softly against the fabric. "Answer me," I say as my fingers curl, beckoning against her sensitive, wet flesh.

A gasp and a weak answer. "Yes."

I shake my head, hands palming her ass and propelling her into my face so I can scrape once, twice, three more times.

"Yes," she cries out.

Her eyes are closed when I reach down and yank her panties in my fisted grip, up so the fabric catches her pussy between the seams. I sink to my knees as she trembles and my eyes line up with the puffy lips that beg to be tasted. I put my mouth on her and she jerks a little. I press my tongue into the cotton and I can already taste her. I let an exhale loose and she squeezes her thighs together, pressing into my face.

I lean back and look at her. "Do you love how I make you feel, *basherte*? Is there any feeling better than this?"

She doesn't answer but it doesn't matter as I shove her body away and back, so she falls on the bed. The moment she hits the mattress, I push her panties to the side and slide my tongue along her wet slit.

Fuck words.

Fuck words the way I'm about to fuck her.

Hard and without a second thought.

Fuck anything that isn't happening in this room with both of us doing whatever feels good.

I push a finger inside her and her back arches.

"Abel," she cries out.

That's me, I think to myself as my tongue flutters over her clit. *That's me making you feel like nothing else matters in this fucked up world.*

"You gonna come, baby?" I ask, sliding my hand under her shirt and bra. When I pinch her nipple, her body shakes.

I put my mouth right back on her center, licking and gripping her thighs, dying to get her close enough to taste every drop.

"Mmm," I hum against her, just as she starts to convulse, her body pushing away. I know it's too much, but I keep going.

I own this moment.

I own her gorgeous fucking body.

But I could never own *her*. I could never count on her as long as she insisted on being this fucked up person. And I should've banked on it because she never promised me she'd ever change.

My dumbass just heard what I wanted to. I let my vision cloud my sight.

She sits up and reaches for me, but I back away, out of her reach.

Unreadable eyes try to assess me, but I look away.

I run my hand over my mouth and sit back on the chair in the corner of the room, not watching as I hear her sit up and adjust herself. From the corner of my eye, I see her reach for her jeans and place them on her lap.

"For a moment, you forgot what you were in love with," she says. "You were just...in love."

"I'm always in love. With you," I tell her with a shake of my head. "I love you so fucking much. But fuck, Rose, you force me to do shit, to be someone I'm not."

There's this quiet consumption, a passing, a digestion of what I've said.

And then there's a truth.

"I don't know that I can change," she says.

Or a version of it anyway.

I hear what the fuck she won't say. I *hear* it and I want to scream at her.

I'm not stupid.

Just because I don't speak the way she does or wasn't brought up in a big ass fancy house, doesn't mean I can't hear that she *won't* change.

"We need to leave," I tell her.

There's a slight shake of her head and then, "I'm not finished here yet."

"I can't stay here. If we get caught, I don't think I could forgive you, Rose." Not any more than I could forgive myself.

"In order for you to forgive me, I'd have to ask for forgiveness. But I'm not sorry, Abel. Not in the slightest."

I stand and shove the chair back, so it hits the wall. "This is fucking bullshit," I say as I grab the keys and walk out, slamming the door behind me.

I run down the steps so fast I nearly trip trying to get the hell away from the wreck inside that room.

What else is left for us?

Will I go back?

Will she even be there if I do?

Once I reach the parking lot, I keep walking. I must walk about half a mile before I get to a gas station. And then I just sit on the bench, watching my breath hit the cold air, watching as it gets darker and darker outside.

The questions that insist on throwing themselves at me, they need to be answered. I can't fucking live with myself if this is all there is. If this is all my future will look like.

Running, hiding, killing.

So I reach in my pocket and pull out my phone.

I scroll down to the number I called before and my thumb hovers over the green button that'll connect me to this condescending asshole.

Don't.

I try to talk myself out of making this call but what the hell else is there for me? I think back to that motel room, to the blood on that girl's hands as she cried at the movie theater, to the cop with the hole in his fucking head.

The scent of tobacco fills my nostrils.

"You knew better than to get tangled up with that *goy*, Abel."

I ignore her, the rasp of her voice, the way it irritates the fuck out of me. And just so I don't have to speak to her, I press the green button.

Every time I try to call this fucking guy, my hands shake. It rings once, twice and by the third ring, I'm nearly ready to hang up.

"Dr. Brown."

That's all this asshole says. Nothing else. I start to think this was a mistake when he speaks again.

"Rose?"

I press my eyes shut and tap the back of my head against the wall behind the bench. "No. It's Abel." I can hear a low buzz of static but that's it.

"Are you with Rose?"

I take a deep breath. I can still smell the tobacco. "Why haven't you called the cops?" Why is he playing with us like this? Why are we getting away with this shit?

"Because I knew when you realized she wasn't capable of giving you the life you wanted, you'd contact me."

"No. I don't want her to go back there," I tell him and my voice sounds fucking shaky and I hate it. I clear my throat. "You hear me? She's not going back."

"You have a better idea?"

He still sounds like a condescending prick but he's all I've got right now.

"She never took her medication," I say. "Maybe if she does…"

"You think I don't know that? The fact that she never even tried to stay on her medication is a testament to her unwillingness to change. Stop listening to her pretty words and her pretty face and pay attention. You're a smart kid, Abel. You know better than this!"

I'd never heard Dr. Brown raise his voice before.

"If she goes back, she'll kill herself," I whisper. He needs to know how serious this is. "That's why I got us outta there. She said if she wasn't out by her birthday, she'd…"

"And you fell into her trap."

"It isn't like that. She loves…"

"What? She loves you? Let me ask you this, Mr. Sommerfeldt. How many people has she attacked since you got her out?" He pauses. "Don't tell me if she's killed anyone because I'll *have* to contact the authorities. They'll shut me down. My reputation will be ruined. In fact, don't tell me anything. Just think of the answer to that in your head. She loves you, but she's willing to jeopardize your newfound freedom. She loves you, but I bet if you asked her to stop, she'd tell you she hasn't finished yet. But don't you see? Her list is never-ending. There is no light at the end of the tunnel. With her, you're in perpetual darkness. Are you prepared to live that way for the rest of your life? Because at some point, this will all catch up to you."

You think that when you hear your fears confirmed, it won't be as bad because you already kinda fucking knew. You think that because you had your suspicions, there would be no way hearing that what you were thinking was true would kill you.

But Dr. Brown is doing more than telling me the truth. He's changing my goddamn future. If I looked five years toward the future, I pictured me and Rose somewhere safe and unbothered and maybe married. Now, I just see me on my knees, cleaning the blood of her latest victim.

"*Far a bisel libe batsolt men miten gantsen leben,*" my ma whispers.

For a little love, you pay all your life.

"Shut the fuck up," I yell. "Both of you."

Dr. Brown sighs on the other end of the phone. "Still hearing your mother?"

I didn't call for this shit. I don't need a therapy session. I don't need to be reminded that the person sitting next to me is all in my head.

I need a cigarette and I need Rose.

I need to feel a little less fucked up.

Before he can say anything else, I disconnect the call and head inside.

"Marlboro Reds," I tell the man behind the counter as I reach for a green lighter.

He doesn't say anything as he reaches for a pack.

I'm dropping cash on the counter when I notice the television in the corner. The dead girl from the movies. Her face is on the screen, along with a number urging anyone who knows anything to call in and report it.

I'm seeing dead people everywhere.

Without a second thought, I step out and light up, relishing in the smoke as it fills my lungs. I'd stopped because I couldn't find money for food, let alone this shit habit.

A few kids are outside playing on skateboards. I hear them cursing and bullshitting and I remember a time when that was my life, coming home late from hanging out with my friends. Or making out with some chick who'd let me get to third base.

I notice their things in a pile beside one of the pumps. There's an iPod sitting on top of a backpack.

I may not be a murderer but I'm still not one of the good guys.

I tuck the iPod into my jacket pocket and head back to the motel. Before I make it there, I light another cigarette and take my time, scrolling through the iPod. Who has one of these things without a passcode? *What a stupid kid.*

I place an earbud in my ear and I am surprised. *Good taste.*

Some music I don't know, but Radiohead comes up and I listen to *Creep* the rest of the way back.

When I reach the steps leading up to our motel room, I crush the cigarette under my heel and stow the iPod in my jacket.

I'm not sure what I expect to see when I open the door, but it isn't Rose with her head tucked against her knees, still no pants on.

I miss the mass of long blonde hair, but I still reach for the shortened strands, unable to keep my hands to myself.

"Why don't you hate me?" she asks, not moving.

"I couldn't if I tried."

She turns her face toward me and those green eyes open me right up.

And I'm reminded of the first lie I ever told Rose.

49 ROSE

Abel doesn't smell like himself as he approaches.

He doesn't look like himself either. His hair is pushed away from his face, as if the minor inconvenience of it was something he didn't care to be bothered with.

He's smiling like he's got some trick up his sleeve.

And when he kisses me, he tastes like kids hiding under the bleachers, pressing against each other, stealing innocence without a second thought.

I should know. I'd made my rounds, the stench of cigarettes clinging to me, even as I'd decided the hit of misbehavior just wasn't enough for me. "Are you my Abel?"

He cocks his head to the side, and his hair slides from his face, the longer strands in front beautiful in their anarchy.

I may look like lightness with all this blonde hair and fair skin, but he is the fairer of the two of us. Fairer in his soul, deep down, where it counts.

Where I'm black as night, he is beautiful and bright.

A beautifully broken man.

"Who else's would I be, *basherte*?"

The suave answer tastes as awful as he does. But I still relax in his presence, content to stop counting. I'd stopped at nine hundred, just as the walls were starting to close in on me.

But they hadn't. I was still here, hours later.

He doesn't wait for me to answer. "I got something." There's still a smile on those lips that made me orgasm not too long ago.

"Oh?"

He shrugs out of his jacket but takes something out of the pocket before tossing it on the chair in the corner of the room. I'm staring at the hand he's hidden from me when he gestures with the free one for me to lie back.

Without a second thought, with all my trust in him, I do as I'm told. His eyes travel, like a caress, down my body, from my white tank top down to my cotton panties that are still damp from earlier.

"There are no words," he says.

And when I think this is about to go in one direction, he surprises me, taking the wheel and lying beside me on the bed.

I notice an iPod in his hand as he unravels the headphones.

"I don't know what you like to listen to, but I swiped this from some kid out there." He clears his throat.

And I ignore that I hate how he smells as he hands me an earbud. "What are we listening to?" I whisper as I press it into my ear.

"Anything. Seriously, anything that will keep us from saying something to fuck this all up."

My eyes are closed before the words are all the way out of his mouth.

I ignore the sound effects in my ear as he makes his way through some stranger's music. The clicking stops and then strings are filling the silence for a moment before a woman's voice starts singing.

"She sounds sad," I say, more to myself than anything.

Abel reaches for my hand and we lie side by side as I listen to this woman singing words I feel all too familiar with.

It's palpable, the circles both our minds are doing in this otherwise empty room. Just our thoughts, our emotions, and our fears suffocating us.

And when the song ends, I squeeze my eyes shut out of fear. *You feel so far from me*, I yearn to say. Instead, I settle for, "Do you regret this?" My mother would disapprove of my lack of clear and concise verbiage, but she's dead now and its only me and Abel here.

"I'm worried I won't be enough," he tells me with a slight squeeze of my fingers. "That one day, all of this will be more important than anything I could ever give you."

The earbud presses painfully into my ear as I shift to face him. Our hands are still clutching each other's, so I bring them up toward my face and kiss his fingers. "My sister killed herself." There isn't a moment's hesitation. Arms envelop me, and every doubt dissipates. "I found her suicide letter in my mother's house."

He presses a kiss to my neck and asks, "She didn't...blame you, did she?" His words are muffled in my skin but his earnestness is heard clearly.

"No." Under the scent of tobacco, is my Abel. I breathe him in again and again before I speak again. "She was raped."

His body stiffens before he sits up, scooting back from me enough to look into my eyes. His eyes are wide, his lips in a tight "o", like he isn't sure what comes next. "Do you know..."

"His name is George. We all went to school together."

"And you've known this all this time?"

"I've been trying to find the best way to explain..."

"That he has to die," he finishes. "And you have to be the one to do it."

Abel's expression is hard to decipher, so I brace myself on my elbows to get a closer look. "Abel..."

"He has to die." There's this resolute understanding in his eyes. "He has to die and then we have to leave."

I don't know that I've loved him more than in this moment.

And I don't know that I've ever wanted to submit to someone

sexually up until this point. Certainly not as strongly as I want to give my whole body to him now.

"I want..." I start, my voice low. But I can't find the nerve inside of me to say it.

"What is it?" Abel's hand reaches out and cradles my face.

I want you to spank me again.

I want you to take my clothes off.

I want...

I pull my shirt off and stare at him before I speak again. "I want you."

50 ABEL

SHE'S SITTING THERE WITH HER PERFECT TITS STARING at me like they belong in my fucking mouth. And I have to fight myself to keep from manhandling her, from shoving my dick inside her like a madman, like some rabid animal until she's screaming.

I want her to be a blank canvas, open to every stroke.

As long as I've waited to have sex with her, I can't deny that it won't be lovemaking. Part of me feels shitty about it but when I look at her, I feel too many things.

Too many things for this to be sweet right now.

She doesn't fight me when I turn her around and push her down to the bed. Or when I pull her panties down over her perfect ass.

I nudge her forward, so her face hits the mattress and her ass is in the air.

My hands are planted on each cheek and one at a time, I slap both before gripping them tightly and pulling her hips back toward my already hard dick. All she needs to do is breathe a certain way and I'm hard for her.

I tug down my zipper and pull my button loose, so my pants sit a little lower on my hips. I grab a condom from my pocket and unwrap it before taking my dick out and placing it on the tip.

With my dick in my hand, sliding the condom over it, I'm staring at her perky little ass and still fighting the urge to shove myself inside of her and lose my goddamn mind.

She's waiting on me. Her hair is fanned out around her and she's waiting for me to fuck her out of her mind.

Because I'm not a heartless fucking prick, I play with her a little, pinching her nipples and rubbing her clit. But even as she's gasping and wriggling, I know it's because my fingers aren't enough. I slide my dick against her slit and her groan is enough for me to stop with the fucking games.

I push inside of her, slowly. So fucking slowly and she's silent but tense, her fingers gripping the bedsheets.

"Oh god," she whispers once I'm all the way inside.

"You okay?" I slide my hand down her spine to the base of her neck.

When she nods, I reach a little higher and grip her hair tight, her strands prisoners in my tight grip. And then I'm moving and each push forward, she rewards me with something. A gasp, a cry, my motherfucking name.

My hips move mindlessly, following some rhythm I can't bother to try to understand. I'm still pulling her hair and she's still making these perfect sounds but now her legs are spread wider and her back is arched and she feels like fucking heaven.

"Fuck." I yank her back hard and reach between her legs, right where my dick is.

It's insane how right this feels, like we were made to fuck each other. She yells out my name as her thighs start to shake and I waste no time pushing faster and harder into her body.

I swear I see fucking spots as I come but I don't stop. Not until my legs damn near give out.

We're both sweaty and out of breath but I can't stop touching her.

I'm running my fingertips over her goosebumps like I can read braille or something.

What would her skin tell me?

Would it tell me I could save her?

ROSE IS asleep next to me when my phone vibrates.

I know who it is without having to look. There's only one person I've called from this phone, other than Rose's burner phone.

I stare at it as it rings and rings.

And then I grab both ends and snap the flip phone in half. I'll have to toss it somewhere soon because we can never be too careful with technology now.

Something as simple as snapping a phone in half, and I've made my choice.

In the darkness of the motel room, I welcome myself to the mayhem.

Mishegas, I hear from the chair in the corner of the room.

I ignore her and turn toward Rose, tucking her into me before falling asleep.

51 ROSE

"ARE YOU SURE YOU DON'T WANT TO SPEND YOUR birthday doing something else?" Abel asks as we enter the costume store.

Our hands swing easily beside each other and he catches the ends of my fingers in his.

"I was kinda hoping I could have you all to myself," he says.

But I see the nervousness in his eyes and the way he glances around. I see his fear and I let him hold onto me in a way that will calm him.

Because I am not the thing that calms him.

I am the thing that makes him *feel*.

We peruse through the racks and Abel stops short.

He's staring at what's been dubbed "Accessories" and his eyes are on the artificial blood. Bags and vials of it.

The vial before me makes my lips twitch.

Abel's fingers press into my shoulder as if he's caught it. "I bet blood makes you so fucking happy."

I wouldn't say *happy*. Maybe something slightly less jovial-sounding. I tap the edge of the plastic that holds the vial inside and watch as it swings back and forth. When I glance at him, I don't see anything other than curiosity in his eyes. With a hint of lust.

And to think, any other man would likely run.

"Both the color and consistency are off. But I suppose so." I turn to walk in front of him toward another section of the store when his right hand catches me, barring my abdomen from leading me away.

"Know what makes me happy?" he asks, his voice lowered to a whisper but potent enough that he could be shouting in my ear.

I glance at him as I lick at the corner of my mouth, slower than I would otherwise. His eyes drop to my lips and I shrug.

"The idea that I could take you into that dressing room over there, cover your mouth with my hand and catch all the noises you make as I fuck you," he says.

It's as if my heart and my feet have somehow been introduced; as if my heart belongs at the soles of my boots. I dissect his words as his stare keeps me from pushing away from him.

"Is that what you did?" I whisper, my cheeks hot from the blush I'm sure I'm wearing. "You fucked me?"

The humor drops from his face and his eyes dart back and forth between mine for a moment. "I mean…"

"What's the difference between fucking and making love?" By now my voice has resumed its natural conversation volume and Abel glances around to see if anyone has heard me.

"With us? Nothing."

"Don't tell me what you think I want to hear, Abel."

His Adam's apple bobs and annoyance shifts his features until he's frowning.

I step out of his reach and move past him to continue searching.

"So, Halloween is in a few days and, what? You're going to find George and off him like some kinda cheesy horror flick?" Abel's voice is quiet as he follows after me.

"Exactly."

People say that Halloween thins the veil between the living and the dead. All I want is to send someone through that veil, to the land of the dead where they belong. Sure, I don't subscribe to these notions. But it's entertaining to play along.

The nearly nonexistent Halloween costumes stare back at me, as if the women modeling them are asking me what I'm doing here. I remember versions of these, distorted in my memories but covering a significant amount of skin. Still, the girls in my school had teetered dangerously on the edge of decency. And some threw decency out the window, happy to show off their bodies.

These costumes, in their cheap plastic covers, have Abel silent beside me.

I see a particular costume has his attention and I reach for it with a grin. "An angel?" I ask. "Perhaps you have no idea who you're dealing with here."

He snorts and grabs the costume from me. "I always heard Lucifer was beautiful." He puts the costume back on the rack with the others. "I never really got it until I met you."

My fingers graze the backs of his hands as he leans in to press a kiss to my cheek.

"I wonder what your ma would think of you saying that," I respond.

Abel's eyes shift just past me before he blinks and is with me once more.

More people have started coming in, and he pulls me close, against his body. It's like he's shielding me from them. Protecting me. But I know better. I know it's the other way around.

"If I'm Lucifer, who are you?" I know we aren't alone. I can almost *feel* eyes skating over us but standing here with Abel makes it feel like that isn't the case. Like we're somewhere private where he could swallow me whole and carry me around forever.

"Just another sinner, I guess. Who fucking knows?" he says, shrugging.

And I follow him as he steps away. I don't need to think about it. My feet move because my body can no longer stand the idea of not being next to his. "And what costume would a sinner wear?"

Abel stops abruptly in front of me and I have to reach out and grab his arms, so I don't knock into him.

"What is it?" I'm peering around him just as he turns his head to smile at me.

"I think I found your costume."

GEORGE ISN'T intelligent by any standard. His areas of expertise are sex and drug paraphernalia and how to score both, if watching him walk inside with bloodshot eyes and a girl on his arm tells me anything.

I'm not sure what Grace would be doing around someone like him but I'm trying not to judge. It's difficult but I'm trying.

I'm no one's victim. I refuse to be. But my little sister isn't like me, so I have to be the one to make things right.

I know Cassandra is having her annual Halloween party. I've passed her house a few times already and I saw kegs being brought in and decorations being hung. I'm itching for night to fall. Itching for Abel to get what he so badly wants. What he's wanted since we escaped Silverwing: to get as far away from here as possible.

I'm sitting in my mother's Mercedes, across the street from George's house. There were rumors before I went away about his family. About his father losing their fortune. The fact that George still drives the same Jeep supports those rumors. Families around here often compete with one another; from the latest cars to the newest appliances, even down to their extra-marital activities.

For men and women who are mostly CEOs and somehow created their own fortunes, their behavior is absolute filth. Because once you mix money and the idea of living a consequence-free life, people turn into monsters worse than even *me*. And don't even get me started on the few "old money" families in this area.

Just as I turn the key in the ignition, George steps out of the house. The same woman he walked in with an hour prior trails behind him, her clothes rumpled and her brown hair messy. It makes me sick to my stomach to see how easily he lives while Grace is dead. He ruined her, and he gets to slap this girl's bottom before she gets in her car and drives away. These thoughts make me want to drive this car up his lawn and right into him. Then reverse and do it again and again until he's unrecognizable.

But that's not the plan. No.

The plan is to wait outside the party until it's in full swing. I can just *feel* the muggy heat of warm bodies, elbow to elbow, as I push my way through to him. These people will stand around as I approach George. I'll attempt to appeal to his libido until I'm close enough to reveal his fate.

"Don't you remember me?" I'll ask him. Because he is of mediocre brain capacity, he'll think we've slept together at some point. But no, George. I am not one of your sex dolls.

"Are my eyes familiar?" I'll ask him when he hasn't figured out who I am. Everyone always said Grace and I had the same eyes. Our father's eyes.

And before I kill him, I'll make sure he knows why this is happening, as I crush his offending sexual organ in my fist. I'll even let him kiss the cool metal before the first bullet leaves the chamber. Kiss the device that'll bring your death. Usher in your end with good faith and a sweet kiss.

He'll get three bullets.

One in the stomach for making me sick to mine.

One in the face for being such a liar.

And one in his groin for raping my little sister.

A hand slides over mine, where I'm still holding the keys in the ignition. Abel attempts to steal my attention as George scratches his genitalia.

"I'm almost done," I say.

"What's the plan?" He's such a force in the passenger seat, but I can't look away.

"Exactly what I figured it would be. These people, they're such a bore. The monotony, nothing ever changes. Even after all this time."

My mother didn't change. George didn't either. It's like they're inviting their fates into their lives, leaving a welcome mat out for their doom.

"This is why we need to fucking leave," Abel answers with an edge in his tone.

I finally look at him, and he takes a moment to grab my face with one hand and kiss me, his tongue and teeth working magically.

And in this moment, I agree. I agree so soundly that I nearly tell him to pack our things, so we can leave now.

But I look at George again and I know. It would be impossible to leave him breathing.

"Let's go," I tell Abel as I pull out of the parking spot.

George stares at me, I can feel his gaze burning into the side of my face. But I don't give him the satisfaction of my eyes.

I'm in a car he knows, and I look a lot like someone he once knew.

But I won't give him the satisfaction of being something other than a ghost.

For now, anyway.

52 ABEL

THERE'S NOTHING LIKE PISSING OUTSIDE, I THINK TO MYSELF AS I shake my dick before tucking it back into my black jeans. I reach for the cigarette I had pinched between my lips to crush it under my heel before I walk back to the car.

"Feel better?" Rose asks from the passenger seat once I get in the car.

She's in a great mood, cheerful as fuck, while I'm somber and on high alert.

One last murder. One more time and then we're out of here.

"Sure," I say.

We've been watching the party since the first guests arrived. It's now in full fucking swing—with the dull thumping of a bass line—but it's not hard to tell a party is going on inside.

I snagged a sack of candy off a kid earlier, like the piece of shit I am. Rose rifles through it and pulls out a lollipop.

"Really?" is the only thing I say when she unwraps it and sticks it in her mouth. I never took her for the candy type.

Or the type to suck on anything with as much enthusiasm as she's showing now.

I make a mental note to introduce her properly to my dick later tonight.

She shifts in her seat and my eyes travel up and down her body, loving how she looks in her black latex body suit with a thigh holster.

Complete with a loaded gun.

It was a good compromise of sexy while still keeping her covered like she requested. A ski mask is half pulled down her face, her blonde hair poking out of the bottom.

She looks sexy as fuck with that lollipop in her mouth.

I don't have much more time to contemplate when she opens the car door.

"Come on, Mr. Sommerfeldt. We're ending someone's life tonight."

We. How terrifying.

"Hold on," I stop her and prop her on the hood of the car.

She leans back as I check her holster one more time, making sure it's secure. Her thigh is smooth against my knuckles and I grab at the flesh there, scooting her closer.

She pulls the lollipop out of her mouth and grips me by the back of my neck, pulling me to her lips for a kiss that tastes like strawberries and my *basherte*.

"Keep it up and I'll spank your ass and take you home," I tell her.

I like to think Rose likes fucking me. The harder I slap her ass, the wetter she gets. The more I pull her hair, the louder she moans. I bite her and she comes. I grab her and yank her around and she shivers with fucking excitement,

Fuck, I never thought I'd meet someone like her. So savage in her own right but so submissive when I demand it. Her body is mine.

My violent girl trusts me to fuck her like it's our last time, every time.

Because who knows? With this life, we never know if it will be.

I only get a smile back as she shoves me away.

She looks so fucking sexy and fun in the black latex suit. She's sucking on that lollipop again like it's my dick and I'm about to yank it from her lips when she hops off the hood of the car.

"Time to do what we came here to do," she says around the stick as she reaches to touch the very real gun sitting in her fake holster.

As we approach the smokers sitting outside the party, no one pays her gun any attention. These dipshits think it's a prop. But they do stare at the way her suit gives just a hint of ass cheek because it's cut so high.

"What are you supposed to be?" some guy yells out, sounding drunk as fuck.

She pulls her lollipop from her mouth and points the candy toward the guy. "The Grim Reaper. I've come to collect."

She stands there as he chuckles, and I'm worried she's gonna take out her gun and empty the motherfucking clip into his chest but she just keeps the lollipop pointed to his chest.

"Bang," she whispers, and then places it back in her mouth before turning to lead us inside.

All I can do is grin at the sight of her ass as she leads us inside. She's nothing like the other chicks I've fucked. They seem so pale in comparison to her.

Any minute now, everyone will be screaming and scattering like cockroaches.

It's muggy, like too many people are crowding the same space. I smell the skunky stench of weed in the air and in the corner, I'm pretty sure two people are fucking. Unless they're doing some sort of humping interpretative dance.

We make our way through and the farther inside we get, the further Rose is from me. It bothers me, like someone's pulled an itchy sweater over me. I tug at my ski mask a little, but there's no relief.

I can only walk a few feet behind her now and wait for chaos to erupt.

I have to trust that she'll get us out of here. Or I'll have to drag her ass out of here, kicking.

These people are all fucked up, dancing without a care in the world. Doing lines and making out. They have no idea what I've unleashed on them. As I stare at the blonde in front of me, with her very real gun, and her crazy ass intentions, I understand that I may as well be pulling the trigger tonight.

I don't do shit like this. *I don't do shit like this.*

And as correct as that may be, I don't stop her. I just watch as she stops, her eyes on someone on the couch.

I recognize him from a few days ago. He's wearing a fucking silk robe, like some lame ass Hugh Hefner wannabe. Golden hair, girls all over him. He looks like the type to get away with murder.

And he has no fucking clue what's headed his way.

I grab what's hopefully a cup full of beer on the table next to me and walk up to Rose.

"Spill this on him," I whisper in her ear as I shove the cup in her hand. "Apologize and turn to walk away." *Who the fuck am I?* I think as I walk to a nearby doorway to watch.

She wastes no time, pretending to stumble, spilling some on him but most on the girl next to him, who gets up and storms off. Rose leans in, I'm guessing to apologize.

When she turns to walk away, it only takes one look of her ass in that suit to get him to yank her back with a grin.

She falls onto his lap.

And she doesn't get up.

In fact, she adjusts herself so she's closer.

It's like I'm watching Rose become someone else. My Rose doesn't sit on strangers' laps. She doesn't even sit on mine unless I put her there. But this Rose has her face so close to this asshole's that I have to fight the urge to pull her off him.

He tries to kiss her but she dodges it.

I don't like it. I don't like how close his dick is to her and I don't like how she smiles as she talks.

I step closer, antsy, hoping this doesn't go south. All I have is a pocket knife and my sheer fucking will to get us the hell out of here.

"Are my eyes familiar?" she asks loud enough so I can hear.

And I smirk. This is just her way of luring him in. There's no fucking way I should be jealous of a guy who doesn't even know he's dead yet.

He tries to push her off him, but she just gets closer, pressing her face against his. She's whispering more shit in his ear and his eyes widen as she reaches between them. Judging by the way he pales, I'd guess she has a good grip on his dick.

Shit, that's gotta suck.

She smiles as she reaches for her gun and I move in even closer to make sure I'll be able to get her out of here once she's done.

"Kiss it," she tells him, and I glance over.

She rubs the butt of the gun over his cheek to his lips and the dumb fuck shakes his head. He tries to yell out, but she presses her mouth against his as she reaches for the ugly ass couch pillow beside them and pushes it between them. When she shoves the gun into the pillow, it's like the world stops.

I can't hear it. I can't even see it, and no one notices when the bullet enters his body. Only the way his body jerks gives it away.

The music, the drugs, and the making out continue and I wonder if it even fucking happened.

It's almost like that stupid fucking question about the tree falling in the woods and no one being around. Did it really happen, then? The guy shouts but by then, Rose is already reaching for my hand and I'm pulling her up.

"Ready?" I ask, my voice louder so she can hear me. I'm confused for a second as she shakes her head.

She pivots and aims for his head, where everyone can see her.

But no one's looking at her. Everyone's dancing and drinking and fucked out of their minds.

Until she pulls the trigger and his brains splatter against the white wall behind him.

And then we're fucking running.

We get outside and I'm holding her hand, just like we did when we escaped Silverwing. *It feels like a fucking lifetime ago*, I think to myself as her hand slips out of mine. I hear people yelling inside and when I look back at Rose, I expect to see her right behind me. But she isn't. She's aiming her gun again, this time at the drunk from earlier.

"Who am I?" she asks him.

He grins as he tells her she's the Grim Reaper. He doesn't realize what the fuck she's capable of.

Not even when I grab her and toss her over my shoulder.

We get to the car and I set her down against the passenger door.

We need to get the fuck out of here but she's pushing against me like she wants to run back inside.

"You don't kill innocent people, remember? What the fuck, Rose?!"

"I didn't get to kill him," she says, her voice sounding choppy. Like she's having the hardest time breathing. "I couldn't…"

"It's not a big deal, Rose. We didn't go to the fucking party for him. You got who you came for and now it's over."

She's shaking her head before the words have left my mouth. "I have to go back."

"Absolutely not. Are you trying to get us caught? Get in the fucking car."

"You don't understand," she shrieks. "There were too many people and George didn't suffer enough. I have to go back."

"You can't change that now. He's dead! The fucker can't feel anything else you'd do to his body. Now get your fucking ass in the fucking car!" I kick the tire next to her and curse a few more times for good measure.

She's pulled off her mask and is tugging her hair and all I want to do is pull her in my arms but I don't know if she'll turn on me. *Ain't that a bitch?*

"You wanna go back? I'd give you the world, Rose. You really wanna go back?" I ask, and she drops her hands and looks up at me.

Her tears have smudged her makeup and there's spots of red here and there. *Blood.* How the fuck am I not disgusted by her violence?

"You'd go back?" She whispers the question carefully.

And it's not like I have a fucking choice in my feelings for her. Not when those beautiful eyes are looking at me like I'm the gate-keeper to all of her dreams. *Fuck me.* "Sure," I shrug. "Yeah. Fine. Whatever."

She hands me the gun and fuck, it surprises me when I start loving the weight of it in my grip. The way the smooth metal slides against my palm.

"Let's go home," she says, and she opens the car door and slides inside.

And as I look around, at the people still making their way out of the house just down the road, I click the safety on and put the gun in my waistband.

One last look before leaving this place forever with my *sheyn royz.*

53 ROSE

ABEL DOESN'T TAKE US HOME. OR, TO THE MOTEL, rather.

He parks the car and faces me with a look so intense, I'm afraid to react at all.

"Are you okay?" he asks as his hands conduct their own search, in spite of my nodding. "He didn't hurt you? I didn't hurt you?"

"No, of course not."

He sits back heavily, so heavy it rocks the car. And then he hits the steering wheel.

I don't know this Abel. I'm unsure of what comes next.

He opens the driver's side door and steps out. I glance around and notice a diner just across the street. Its lights are on and there are a handful of people inside.

All while Abel paces around outside, I watch the people inside, wondering if I'll ever be like them.

Or if I'll only ever be a slave.

To my love.

To my violence.

To my rage.

My door opens and Abel yanks me out.

"Come on," he says as he starts walking.

"Where are we going?" I call out from behind him as he drags me by my arm. It doesn't hurt. He'd never hurt me. But there's a small flare inside my chest that I have to swallow down.

I am, after all, coming down from an extremely violent high. If I fall back into it, it's unlikely I'll be able to smother that flame again.

"We're getting breakfast," he tosses over his shoulder as we head to the diner. I notice that at some point, he pulled off his ski mask, and his disheveled hair is now blowing in the wind as we rush toward the diner.

It's cold and I regret not bringing a change of clothes with me. I regret it even more when we walk inside and one of the older waitresses squints at the look of us.

We sit in the nearest booth and I look around, taking in the rundown place.

When my eyes reach Abel again, he frowns before licking the end of one of the napkins on the table and wipes at my face.

Blood.

Victory's nectar.

"Thank you."

He folds the napkin up and places it in his pocket. "You're beautiful, *basherte.*"

I warm under his compliment, a smile spreading on my heated cheeks.

"What'll you be having?" the waitress asks.

Abel orders food and I tuck my feet under my thighs.

I can feel her stare. It reminds me so much of the eyes at Silverwing. The ones that could touch you.

She walks away, and Abel grabs my hand, stroking my fingers with the tips of his. "Where should we go next?"

"I never imagined myself anywhere other than Silverwing," I say.

Or killing my mother and finding Grace.

But they're both gone now.

"I like the idea of getting out of America," he announces.

I smile at our joined hands. "That is likely the smartest idea," I respond.

He drops my hand and stands.

I wonder what's going on for a moment but then he slides in the booth next to me.

Empty hands reach for me like I was meant to fill his empties with my brimming ways.

"What does it feel like?" he asks. There's a tremor in his voice. It's nearly undetectable, hanging on the ends of his words like an unwanted tag-along.

"To take someone's life?" I feel the need to uncover the moment for what it is: Abel becoming less and less repulsed by the things I do and more curious.

As if he knows I'm forcing him to face the question for what it is, he nods once, swiftly and easily missed by someone who doesn't watch him like they exist to do so.

I sit back but turn my head. I need to see his face as I describe this, even if just his profile. "There's this anticipation. I can hardly explain it other than to say there's such a thrill in the hunt. The moments leading up are like…"

"Foreplay?" he asks as he places his hand on my bare thigh.

"I can't relate," I answer and the tremor that'd plagued Abel's words find mine.

"I know you could, *basherte*," he tells me and that hand slides higher. "I know you could."

My mind blanks just as I part my lips and let out a sigh. His fingers are pressed against my sex and moving in a way that makes it impossible to think.

"Nothing feels like this," I whisper. The truth comes easily when coaxed by such talented fingers. I slide toward him and press my face into his neck.

"Nothing?"

I gasp as he pinches me before rubbing those dangerous circles again. He does it once more and I shake my head, quick jabs of movement that punctuate the moments of high ecstasy.

"What if we did this every day instead?" he asks.

My arms move to push myself away from him but he's ready for the reaction, holding me against him, arms banded around me.

"Calm down, Rose."

He whispers the words into my hair as I jerk away from him, only for him to hold me tighter.

"Come on, *basherte.*"

He taints that word with his false acceptance.

I give one more good push and give up when he doesn't budge. I could bite him. I could bash my head into his. I could keep fighting. But I can't do any of these things.

In my love, I am weak.

"If we stay here...damn it, Rose. Listen to me!"

I'm writhing in his arms and by the time I stop, we're both out of breath.

"If we stay here, we'll get caught," he says. "And then there's no way in hell we could ever be together."

"I'd never get us caught."

"You killed a fucking cop!" he says.

"I *knew* you were still upset about that."

"It's not about..."

"Then why bring it up?" I'm still raw from that night; still feeling the cool metal of the gun against my temple.

"Because you aren't as careful as you think you are." He looks past me at the muted television.

And I look, just in time to see the cop car being pulled from the water, a reporter saying words I can't hear. But I don't need to hear her to know that our situation just got a little shaken up.

"Your food's ready," the waitress announces as she sets plates down in front of us.

Abel thanks her and slides back, opposite me.

And that may be all. That could've been the end of it, but I see the waitress watching us.

"She's figuring something out," I whisper before taking a bite of my omelet.

Abel, still chewing, looks back at her, only for her to look away and pretend to wipe something. "You're being paranoid. She probably just thinks we're gonna bail on the bill."

"And if we have to kill her?" I ask.

"Jesus Christ, Rose. This isn't some fucking game. Some murderous fucking adventure. This is my life, Rose. My *life*. And I offered it to you, no questions asked."

"You think life on the run is meant to be some sort of fairytale, Abel. And that seems to be the problem here because I've never offered you anything other than what I am. So if you can't do this anymore, walk away." I stab at my eggs in frustration, an emotion I have no patience for. "Because I can't take you expecting me to change and then being disappointed when I don't."

I don't look at him. I don't let him know that if he left me, I'd be right back to counting the rest of my days away in a cell.

Abel is my last bit of humanity.

"I'm sorry. You're right." He sets his fork down with a *clink* and leans forward to stop my hands from their angry movements. "I'm sorry and I love you."

54 ABEL

I'VE JUST APOLOGIZED TO ROSE WHEN SOMEONE approaches the table. I expect the waitress, but when I look up, there's a man in front of us—homeless, from the looks of it. The waitress is nowhere in sight.

"You guys eatin' real good over here," he says.

I nod and watch Rose.

"Got a dollar?" he asks.

"Sorry, man." I shovel some eggs in my mouth.

"Don't be greedy, kid."

Rose sits silently across from me, her eyes on her breakfast. Is she tuning him out? Part of me wants to pray for that to be the truth but she's chewing a lot slower than she was before.

"Come on, I know you got a dollar," the man insists.

I shake my head.

"Your future is less and less certain the more time you spend here, badgering us for some money that we will never give you," Rose says to him.

It isn't what she says that has me choking on my coffee. It's her emotionless monotone and the way the old man pauses for a moment like she'd been speaking Yiddish.

"Fuck you," the man says.

And I reach for Rose's hand but it's too late. She's already got the fork poised in the air and then diving it until it's sticking out of the man's fucking hand.

He screams, and I set a hundred on the table before grabbing Rose. As we're running, she stumbles and before I can think about it, I swoop her into my arms and jog us the fuck out of there.

And just like every other time, I'm saving her ass.

If that isn't love, what the fuck is?

I could never leave Rose behind again. Not after everyone else left her in fucking Silverwing. I will not let her believe that she doesn't deserve love just because she isn't perfect.

I'd never let her die thinking no one loved her.

Because I love Rose through her evil. Maybe even in spite of her evil.

Nah. I shake my head.

I just love her. Even with the crazy fucking madness around us.

I've come to love every fucking crack in Rose as much as I love the perfect parts of her. She makes it impossible for me to not love every single thing about her.

I've learned to love the way she looks with blood on her hands and a gun in her waistband. I love how easily she brings the monster out of the man.

"You crazy woman," I yell with a laugh. "I'm in love with a crazy woman!"

I hadn't noticed the rain until we stepped outside. Having to carry Rose is slowing me down but I get her to the car and make sure she's in before I open my door. Just as I'm about to put the key in the ignition, her door opens, and the homeless guy is pulling her from the car.

She cries out as he tugs her hair and drags her over the gravel.

I don't think.

I pull out the gun in my waistband.

I switch the safety off.

And I shoot.

No one touches Rose.

No motherfucker in this world will ever touch her and live to talk about it.

It's like I blacked the fuck out, and all I can hear is my ma.

Look at what this shikse's done to my boy.

But she doesn't understand.

My Rose leaves a trail of thorns and dead bodies behind her.

And she saves her petals for me.

One day I'll end up with a shitty mess of a heart and a pocket full of thorns.

But until then, it's us against the world.

The man is lying on the gravel, his body looking still in the dark. I hadn't realized that as I was shooting, I was walking closer and closer until I was standing over him.

Rose peers at him from behind me, curiously.

It's unnerving.

There's something about the smell of gunpowder in the rain. It's sharper and I can almost taste it, like I'd sucked on the end of the barrel after it went off.

There's something about a dead body in the rain. Like maybe their god was washing away the sins of their life and I was somehow caught in something that didn't belong to me.

There's something about the way I am now.

I'm a fucking murderer.

I was always such shit at poetry but this comes to mind like I'd been thinking it for months. Maybe I had.

Roses are red.

Violence is cool.

Abel is sweet.

Abel's a fool.

55 ROSE

In Abel's violence, he is magnificent, and I am perpetually smitten.

Blood is beautifully splattered on his alabaster skin as if placed by some divine artist; someone with a hand only a god could have designated. Blood is paint and his weapon is the paint brush. Life is our endless canvas.

Even under the dim streetlights, I can see it start to wash away under the rain.

"We're artists," I murmur.

Abel glances over at me and pulls me into his arms. "Are you hurt?"

I shake my head, with an urgent wanting to feel his lips against mine. He doesn't disappoint.

We are ravenous in our victory.

In my love, I am a fool.

In his love, he is my protector.

I wanted to be perfect, just so he could ruin me, but he ended up being the one ruined.

I'm the beast to his beauty.

I am his prisoner and he is mine.

In our love, we will perish.

I hear the sirens before I see them, and we break apart to get in the car. We're speeding down the street, just as they've pulled up to the diner.

I watch them in the rearview mirror, my pulse hammering.

"It's okay, Rose." He kisses my knuckles. "We're okay."

We speed the rest of the way to the motel. No words are shared between us. The feeling of something ominous breathing down our necks keeps us silent.

"Get upstairs and start packing," Abel directs me as he reaches for something in his pocket.

I see the pieces of his phone in his hand and I pause, confused.

"Go, Rose."

I run up the steps and get everything I can, jamming them into bags and even a few pillowcases.

When Abel comes in, he shakes his head. "You're efficient, that's for fucking sure," he says with a chuckle.

We take turns loading our things into the car and then we're gone.

I'd like to say without a trace but leaving a hotel room you've lived in for weeks without notice tends to be a little messy.

Still, Abel handles everything and as he pumps gas, I wonder what happened to his phone. When he gets back in the car, I ask.

"How did you break your phone?"

The shrug is nonchalant, but the words feel so forced. "I got upset."

Having borne witness to his anger recently, I nod and leave him be.

I'm asleep when we reach a destination that has Abel shaking me awake. He hands me the gun and I tuck it into the front of my bodysuit, too exhausted to care about who may see it.

"Come on," he says as he presses a kiss to my cheek before leading me to the room he'd checked us into while I slept. "Stay here. I'll get our things."

I stash the gun on the shelf in the closet. Then I sit on the bed, but I can't sleep. So, I watch Abel come in and out until he's finished. And then he starts to organize our things, as if we're staying here. "Where are we?"

"New Jersey," he informs me. "Somewhere we haven't been before."

Somewhere they won't look for us. Somewhere the trail of dead bodies won't lead.

I hear all the words.

"Go back to sleep."

"I can't." And I'm yearning to release myself from this uncomfortable suit I've trapped my body in. "I have to take this off. I feel disgusting."

"You don't look it," he says with a grin.

I start to pull at the zipper in front and Abel stops for a moment, watching me. When I've taken the suit completely off, he focuses once again on the clothes.

"Do you like it when I'm naked?" I ask him.

"Do you like it when I slap your ass?" he counters, taking his eyes away from the clothes he's folding to stare at me. Perhaps he thinks he can read my mind the way I've always wanted to read his.

"If I didn't, you'd be dead," I answer. I snag one of the white t-shirts and pull it on.

His smirk is like a wrecking ball to my defenses. I should be careful. I shouldn't love him to the point of pain.

It's too late.

"You like pain? Or is it just that it's me?" he asks.

I remember bringing up my past sexual encounters when we escaped Silverwing. That was the last time I'd ever even eluded to my sexual history. "I couldn't be certain but I'm thinking it may just be you."

He sets one of his t-shirts down and leans forward, elbows against the ironing board for a moment. That moment is all it takes to make my skin tingle, especially that place between my thighs.

The way Abel's eyes are glued to my chest makes me think he can see the way my nipples have tightened.

"Then how about I don't fuck you right now?"

It feels like my heart has left my body when he says this. "No sex?" I lick my lips, straightening, confused because I don't remember when I'd started to lie back. *The moment he looked at you with those eyes that see everything.*

"No fucking," he corrects me. He's standing in front of me and then he's bending at the waist, following me all the way until I'm lying on my back. "Think I can taste you without going fucking crazy, *basherte?*"

I keep my wide eyes on his, even as he breaks the contact.

His fingers pinch the hem of my shirt and his eyes are greedy on the flesh he's revealed. "Want to try?"

My nod is eager. In my need for Abel, I am eager and terrified.

"Should I start," he presses a kiss to my chin, "here?"

I shake my head.

"No?"

I watch the top of his head, admiring the light brown locks as he pulls my shirt over my breasts before settling the fabric over and into my mouth and then shoving it between my teeth. Warm wet suction envelopes my nipple and I arch my back with a groan.

"What about here? Is this a good place to start?"

I'm nearly gnawing on the fabric as I shake my head and slide my feet down the mattress.

"No?"

He's quiet as he keeps my shirt against my mouth, the other hand struggling to remove my panties. He loses his patience and ducks under and into the space between my body and the layer of cloth he'd tried to rid me of.

One of my knees is on his shoulder and he curses before pressing his mouth to my body.

I feel the shriek build in my chest and work its way up.

"Can I start here?" he asks as he looks up at me and licks his lips.

I'm trying to catch my breath and he takes my lack of words as consent.

The orgasm is instantaneous.

Abel shoves inside me and his soon follows. We're a mess of euphoric tingles, this high that nothing can touch.

This high is love, and yet the worst things can come of it.

We do terrible things for the people we love.

And I would do the worst for him, just for a moment like this.

We gave our love away so freely to each other. Something sacred given without thought or reservation. It was as effortless as existing. I exist and so I love Abel Sommerfeldt.

We give love for free and yet we want the world in return.

"Do I make you feel safe?" He whispers the question across my skin like he's trying to slip the words past my pores and into my soul.

Still, I shake my head. "I make myself feel safe. You just make life bearable in my soi-disant safety."

He grabs me and pulls me against him so my bottom sits against his groin.

I want to jerk away at the feel of his returning erection, but I don't. Not when the last thing I want is space between us.

"What's that mean?" Another whisper, this time in my hair.

I blink a few times in the darkness. "It means I should never be without you. It means I'm never going back. Promise me you'll end my life before that ever happens."

I expect an immediate answer, one aimed for my heart to soothe the ache that threatens to paralyze me.

But there's only dark silence. So silent, I can hear the music from the lobby, a few doors away from us.

"That something you think about a lot?" he asks. The silence gives way to the edge of fear in his voice, betraying his emotions.

"Do you think about it at all?" I wonder aloud.

"Of course," he tells me as he squeezes me tighter, nearly to the point of pain. "I can hardly breathe if I think about it for too long."

I inhale, deeply and steadily, feeling the way my chest tightens and my breath hitches. He's holding me so close he must feel my momentary tremor. "You love a mad, mad woman, Abel," I whisper and turn in his arms. I can feel his exhale against my face just as I inhale again. His exhale, my inhale; his air becomes mine as he presses a kiss to my cheek.

"Eh. She's not so bad."

56 ABEL

Rose still sleeps when I can't. But I can't find it in me to wake her up just because insomnia is kicking my ass.

I turn on the TV and flip to the nearest news channel.

And then my world is flipped upside down.

Rose's face is on the screen, with a number to call. Though the television is muted, when her mother's face pops up, I know we're fucked. I turn the volume up just a little.

They've traced the car back to her mother. They found the cop car. They're even pinning what they've dubbed "The Halloween Shoot-Out" on her. The reporter continues to urge anyone who might have information to call the hotline number. And not only does she say it, but it is scrolling along the bottom of the screen. Before she's finished, I've memorized the fucking number without even attempting to.

The reporter never mentions my name.

My mind wanders to Joe, wondering why he hasn't reported me as missing.

Suddenly, I'm a flurry of activity, picking things up and throwing them into the bags we'd *just* taken them out of.

"Why are you packing?" Rose's groggy voice cuts through my internal chaos.

I stop and stare at her with wide eyes. "We need to get the hell out of here." I gesture toward the TV.

"There's no need..."

"No. No! I'm done listening to you right now. I know a thing or two about surviving and if we keep doing whatever the fuck you want, we'll end up walking right back into Silverwing." I drop the clothes in my hands and take the few steps separating us.

Her face is in my hands and I look at her, not blinking. When I press my lips to hers, hard, she opens her mouth to my coaxing but I pull away before it can turn into anything more.

"I fucking love you," I tell her. "I have nothing but that. It's the most valuable thing I'll ever have. All I can do is tell you that I'm yours. I'm fucking yours and it's gonna be just you and me for a while. Sometimes you'll have to listen to me because we're partners. You're my equal." I grin, not minding how crazy all of this sounds. "Hell, most days you're the fucking boss and I'm just here to do whatever it is you want. But sometimes you need to listen to me. You got me?"

She nods and I'm not sure what comes next, where we'll go next. But I'm ready to go wherever she does.

"You curse so much. I know you're smart but nobody else would." Her words sting, and she smiles. "Let them underestimate you."

She gets in the shower as I finish packing.

I'm placing everything by the door when I hear a knock. I hesitate because *what the fuck?* Who would be coming to see us?

"Who is it?" I ask, attempting to deepen my voice. I'd let Rose bring the gun in, not wanting to touch that shit again after last night and now I have no idea where she put it.

"It's the manager."

I open the door a crack and meet a pair of stern brown eyes.

"Sir, open the door..."

"What for? We've paid, same as everyone else, for some privacy."

"Yeah, well, we were tipped off that there may be a suspect wanted for murder in the area, so we're taking a look."

I squint a little in response.

She places her hand on the door. "You either let me in, or the police will be called."

I sigh as I open it, praying Rose stays quiet and inside the bathroom.

"You the only one in here?"

I nod as she eyes our things.

"Looks like you're all packed and ready to go."

"At a moment's notice, not that it's any of your concern. We done here?"

The manager looks around once more with a nod before heading toward the door.

And just as we're almost in the clear, Rose steps out of the bathroom in a towel.

The woman takes one look at her and her eyes look like they're about to pop out of her damn head.

I slam our door shut and before I can think, I'm yanking the motel manager to me and holding my hand over her mouth. Rose jumps over the bed and reaches in my jacket for my knife. And before I can talk her into or out of anything, she's stabbing the woman over and over, so many times that her blood is now covering Rose's towel.

I call her name, but she doesn't stop.

And so I make a dumb as shit decision and hold my hand up.

Hot pain shoots up my arm all the way to my goddamn elbow and straight to my shoulder as the knife slices into my palm. Only when I grunt does Rose stop thrashing and really fucking look at me.

Blood is already dripping down to the floor, making these little splatters that I can't stop staring at. But I manage to look her in the eye somehow and she's staring at me strangely, her lips parted a little, eyes wide as fuck.

She grabs my injured hand, not giving a shit about all the blood. "No," she whispers before yelling, "No!"

She's about to hit the floor but I toss the dead woman aside and grab her. There's so much fucking blood. It's everywhere.

"I never wanted to hurt you," she sobs.

"I know, baby." I rock her in my arms for a moment before trying to lift her but she's inconsolable.

And then I hear it.

The sound of our end.

Sirens wail in the distance as I try to pick Rose up to carry her. But she's clawing at me, jerking her body away from me, moaning words that I can't understand as tears fill my eyes.

"Rose, they're going to fucking kill us."

She drops to the floor, determined to stay in this room.

The sirens make it so hard to hear her words but by the third time, I know what she's telling me.

"You have to kill me."

I shake my head, one quick jerk to get her to shut the fuck up so I can think.

I can't think when she says that shit.

Like I can live in this fucking world without her?

"Abel," she shouts before grabbing my head between her hands. "You take that gun and you blow my brains out or I'll do it myself."

"No," I say before pulling away from her. "Bring me the fucking gun, Rose." I hold my hand out.

But she scoots away, putting space between us like I won't just grab her again.

And I do, yanking her against me and breathing hard. "Stop it! Stop it!" I grind out as she fights me. "Trust me! For God's sake can you just try to trust me? I can fix this. I can make this go away!"

She shakes her head and runs into the closet. I'm trying to pull it open but she's fighting so hard.

And I know. She had to have put the gun in there.

"Rose," I scream. "Rose, baby. Don't do this!"

I hear footsteps outside the door. My knees almost buckle at the sound of them. I finally get the door open and Rose has the gun in her hand, aimed at the ceiling, tears running down her beautiful face.

"Say goodbye," she says.

A small smile touches her lips for a moment as I rush toward her.

But she brings the gun to her temple just as the sound of the door being knocked from its hinges makes me jump.

I look away from her for just a moment as they rush in, guns up and shields protecting them from us. The bullets aren't for these fuckers. Not when she plans on putting one in her brain. I'm turning to see her when I hear it.

Bang.

But I can't look because I'm already being dragged out of the room.

IT FEELS like I'm missing a piece of myself. Like one of these fuck heads cut off my arm and I'm bleeding out. But I'm not bleeding, and nothing is missing. I glance down at my cuffed wrists and I even go as far as to wiggle my toes.

Looking up at the hairy motherfucker in front of me, I accept that not all wounds are physical. The mortal wounds are the ones that turn your insides cold and make you yearn for something you never knew you even fucking *had*. I almost wish someone would cut off my arm, just so I'd have something to take my mind off the panic coursing through my body.

"I'll ask you one more time…"

"Where is she?" I ask.

"At the fucking morgue! She put a bullet in her brain for God's sake."

My head shakes before he's even finished. "No. You're wrong. Rose...she...she wouldn't. You're wrong!" I yell, spit flying from my mouth. "You lying motherfuckers!"

"You and that fucking psycho went on a killing spree. You'll be spending the rest of your life behind bars. You think I give a *shit* enough to lie to you, boy?"

I can't help the tears. And all this fat motherfucker does is sigh, stand up, and tell me to get comfortable.

All while my ma smokes in the corner of the room, flicking her ashes at him and nodding with a look of disgust on her face.

I told you, idyot, is all she says.

EPILOGUE
ABEL

THE METAL CLANGING OF THE PRISON CELL OPENING snaps me out of my daydream. It was a really fucking good one, too.

Rose was sitting next to me, alive, and as beautiful as she'd always been.

I glare at the asshole guard with a grunt. My body is harder now, marked by the fuckers in here that had tried me. But they didn't know I wasn't a pussy anymore. I embraced the fight. Fuck them. Shed blood.

Rose would be so fucking proud.

When they hand me the clothes I was wearing when I was sentenced, I shake my head. There's no fucking *way* I'll fit in those now. But I go ahead and put them on, anxious to get the fuck out of here.

I don't have a plan, but anything has to be better than this.

"Nice pants, Abe," one of the guards says as I walk past.

The urge to shove my foot up his ass is only a little weaker than my need to be out.

"Ready?" the female officer in front of me asks.

I nod my head once and the doors open.

The sight of an empty parking lot meets me and even though I know no one will be waiting for me, it's still a kick in the chest when I see it for myself. I rub my hand over my heart as I walk through the parking lot, toward the bus stop. I have no fucking clue where I'm going but I'm not staying here.

After a few minutes, I hear the bus rumbling toward me. Its brakes squeal as I shake the change I found in my old wallet around in my closed fist.

"How much?" I ask as I climb on.

The driver shoots me a look. Like he knows what I've done and where I've been. "Dollar fifty," he says.

I push the change into the slot and take the closest free seat.

All the anxiety I should be feeling is nowhere in sight. I'm calm as fuck. That should freak me out. Last time I'd been out, everything had gone to hell.

Mishegas, mishegas.

This time it's my voice in my head.

It was the happiest I'd ever fucking been.

Not hearing my ma anymore certainly helped. Dr. Brown's testimony helped even more after he insisted it was all Rose, that I'd only been her floozy.

I didn't like it. But I took it.

And six years later, I'm free.

I stand to get off, the only one wanting to get off at this stop. I feel the driver's glare but fuck him. Fuck this bus. Fuck this life.

I take a few steps and the anxiety starts crawling up my fucking neck.

And then I hike. It feels like miles before I reach my destination.

Everything looks the same. Everything except the sign for Silverwing has been removed. You can still make out the letters against the brick from years of wear around it.

But Silverwing doesn't exist anymore.

They've built around it, and it stands tall, proud of all the terror that once lived there. It's no wonder no one's done shit with it.

I stare at this building that doesn't mean shit to the dozens of people on the sidewalk, now that they've built a strip mall around it. They have no fucking clue what happened here.

Was it magic or was I just another dumb *schmuck*?

If I think hard enough, I can remember what she was like, even down to the way she smelled. Sweet, without perfume to cover it up.

The breeze kicks up and my eyes are closed but I smell her. I smell her like she's right fucking next to me.

If I wished hard enough, would I wake up from this nightmare?

I open my eyes slowly and...

Rose is standing in front of me, wearing that fucking smile, the one that gets us into trouble.

"Blood is red," she starts as she steps closer, "death is true..."

I smile as she touches her fingers to my arms.

She feels so real.

"Abel, my love, we've got more killing to do."

I close my eyes again and count to five.

When I open my eyes, she's still in front of me, only she isn't touching me.

The same smile, the same eyes, the same everything.

She reaches up and her fingers grip the collar of my shirt for a second. They let go as she leans in. I can still smell her like she's right here, but she can't be. She's fucking dead. They told me.

"You're dead," I whisper.

She shakes her head. "No. Everyone else is."

ACKNOWLEDGMENTS

I typically write my acknowledgements about halfway through, so I don't have to do what I'm doing now.

Scrambling at 11:46 at night, deadline ready to punch me in my face with Bella Swan on my TV in the background, all sad because Edward Cullen left and shit.

What I'm trying to say is, no one wants to be that asshole they see at awards shows, forgetting important people. So, Bella has to be quiet for a sec while I do this (#TeamEdward).

First and foremost, if I hadn't written EVOL, I wouldn't have finished this book that's been sitting on my laptop for years. EVOL brought me back to life and gained me so many people who then pushed me to finish this book.

I'm forever grateful for the cycle that this life continues on.

Thank you to Jen Rogue. You are the bravest and the most emotionally fearless woman I know. Let it all hang out and let the fucking world love you for it.

Kat, you saved my ass when I'd decided I would never find the right cover for this book. You knocked this cover outta the damn park, lady.

Muhfuckin' Christina. Part of me doesn't even want to write

anything about you because NONE OF IT will do justice. You are the best cheerleader/editor/fellow Abel lover that I've ever known. Full of unwavering support and you don't mind my dumb ass voicemails. Can I squeeze you again? K, thanks.

Talon. Beta extraordinaire. So glad you put up with my erratic timeline and didn't tell me to fuck off. You have my heart. Mainly because we can talk books in one breath and in the next, discuss the latest hip hop beef. You are the realest to ever do it.

Enakshi and Lisa, you gals gave me life while I was able to give you chapters on time. Sorry I suck. So glad you two don't!

Ace Gray, you are BAE! Your kindness…man, you're epic. I wish the entire world was like you, but it makes sense that you're one-of-a-kind, unicorn lady. Thanks for always offering an ear.

Shout out to the Sayers. Especially the ones who've been with me from the beginning. You know the drill. The story never ends here.

To my family, thanks for letting me be the weird one. I am blessed to be able to express myself so freely.

I want to take a moment to thank myself. For letting myself set this book aside until I was ready to do it the right way. For letting myself *feel*, even when all I felt was fear. And for letting the universe lead me, even when I didn't trust that I was going the right way.

And lastly, to the music. It can set you free.

ABOUT THE AUTHOR

Cynthia hates writing her own bio. In her down-time, you can find her watching movies, ranging anywhere from classic to action flicks (she has a weakness for Marvel adaptations), and reading any novel she can get her hands on.

She loves hearing from her readers! You can reach Cynthia at cynthia.a.rodriguez6@gmail.com, & her website, where she blogs about books, writing, and leaves really great song suggestions.

EIGHT YEARS LATER
ABEL

My palm aches most days. That's what getting stabbed will get you.

Hard labor brings out all the goddamn aches. It reminds me just how old my body feels. Prematurely, I'd say. But fuck it. I'm still free and that has to mean something.

At the factory, most of the guys leave me alone. Some try to talk, and I humor them for a few moments. But I like my fucking solitude. Less to explain that way.

I step inside my apartment, ready to reheat some leftover pizza and catch the new episode of Game of Thrones when I pause, still rubbing the scar on my palm.

My dog usually greets me at the door, but my place looks empty. No sign of him.

"Marco?" I even whistle but he doesn't come. "Marco?" I call out again.

The apartment is dark, and I've got this creepy ass feeling that I can't shake.

What the fuck is going on?

I turn on the light in my bedroom and there he is, sitting on my bed.

Mishegas.

Right next to Rose.

"Ready?" she asks, her feet tucked under her ass.

She looks the same, like a perfect angel, while I've aged and grown tired.

She is everything I'm not. Perfect, still young, still vibrant.

And she brings out the monster in me.

"I'm tired," I say, as if I'm speaking to myself. But I know better, even as I'm crossing the room to sit on the bed, my back to her.

I know with every day that passes that I don't take the medication I was prescribed, I'm risking lives.

But on those days…I don't feel alive. I don't see Rose and when she slips away, part of me dies with her.

So, it's us against the world. All over again.

"Let's go get a girl," she whispers, climbing over the bed to sit next to me. "That was fun last time."

But it wasn't.

Once it'd all been said and done, Rose was gone, and I had to get rid of her body alone. I was sick for days afterward, unable to look at myself.

And it forced me to take those goddamn pills for a month straight afterward.

But I always came back to Rose. And she always welcomed me with open arms, never angry at me for being away for too long.

"I can't do this anymore," I whisper. And I feel so fucking alone, speaking out loud in this room where only my dog can hear me.

Because Rose isn't really here.

Tell that to my fucking heart.

"I love you, but I can't," I tell her, trying not to sob, trying not to feel like I'm constantly letting her down. "I tried to save you but I'm killing myself in the goddamn process."

And other people.

But saying that out loud? No way. I had to keep a lid on my

guilt, or it would come out and swallow me whole like Jonah's fucking whale.

No one would save me if I drowned. No one is here.

So, I grab my pills and pop two in my mouth.

Soft hands, I swear I can feel them on my back.

I hear her whispering that she loves me as I let myself sink into a deep sleep.

If you love me, set me free...

Made in United States
Orlando, FL
12 October 2023